MORRIS AUTOMATED INFORMATION NETWORK
0 1029 066346
W9-AUW-197

FIREBRAND

FIREBRAND

AARON BARNHART

Adapted from the novel
Border Hawk: August Bondi
by Lloyd Alexander

QUINDARO PRESS  KANSAS CITY

For my nephews
Alexander Newman and Jesse McFarlane
who served their country

Firebrand
Quindaro Press
Kansas City, Missouri
QuindaroPress.com
ISBN 978-0-9669258-6-9
Library of Congress Catalog Number 2015942156
Summary: In 1848 Vienna, fifteen-year-old August Bondi is forced to emigrate to America, leaving behind his comrades in the revolution. In his new country he is confronted by the evil of slavery, and sets out for Bleeding Kansas to join forces with the notorious John Brown. Adapted from *Border Hawk* by Lloyd Alexander and based on Bondi's autobiography; includes maps and historical note.

Some portions previously appeared in Alexander, Lloyd, *Border Hawk: August Bondi* (Jewish Publication Society, 1958).
Cover design by Kelly Carter
Set in Calluna and Rosewood
Printed in the United States of America by Worzalla
Distributed by Itasca Books, Minneapolis, Minnesota

10 9 8 7 6 5 4 3 2 1

INTRODUCTION

Imagine living the first fourteen years of your life in a police state. Every word you and your parents say in public can be used against you. Because you never know who might be a spy — a neighbor, a so-called friend — you keep your opinions to yourself. If your father's business gets a visit from a local official demanding a bribe, he pays it. If your mother hears someone insulting her people, she bites her tongue and says nothing. As for you: Do as you're told, for everyone's sake.

That was the world as fourteen-year-old August Anschl Bondi knew it. He was born in 1833 in the Jewish section of Vienna, Austria, to Martha and Herz Emmanuel Bondi. The country was ruled by Prince Klemens Wenzel von Metternich, a tyrant who did not allow freedom of the press, freedom of assembly, or freedom of speech. In the United States, these liberties were written into the Bill of Rights forty years earlier. News traveled slow in those days, but not that slow. Metternich simply felt he could rule as princes had ruled for centuries, and he was not alone. Much of Europe was the domain of monarchs whose form of government looked ancient compared with American-style democracy.

In 1848, when Anschl was fourteen, a wave of protests swept across the continent. From Paris to Prague, Milan to Budapest, huge rallies were held as people demanded a say in how their societies were governed. Students led many of the demonstrations. Anschl was at the center of the rebellion in Vienna. The events of 1848 changed everything for the Bondi family. They would be forced to leave Europe for America, where August Bondi (as he began to call himself) returned to the fight for freedom in his new home of Kansas, joining forces with the notorious opponent of slavery, John Brown.

The following novel is fictionalized from real stories taken from the life of August Bondi. As you read it, think of other people you may have read about who were treated badly because of who they are or what they believe. August Bondi was not a superhuman figure. He was an ordinary teenager caught up in extraordinary times, and as people around him began taking sides, he was forced to make the decision of his life.

ANSCHL'S WORLD

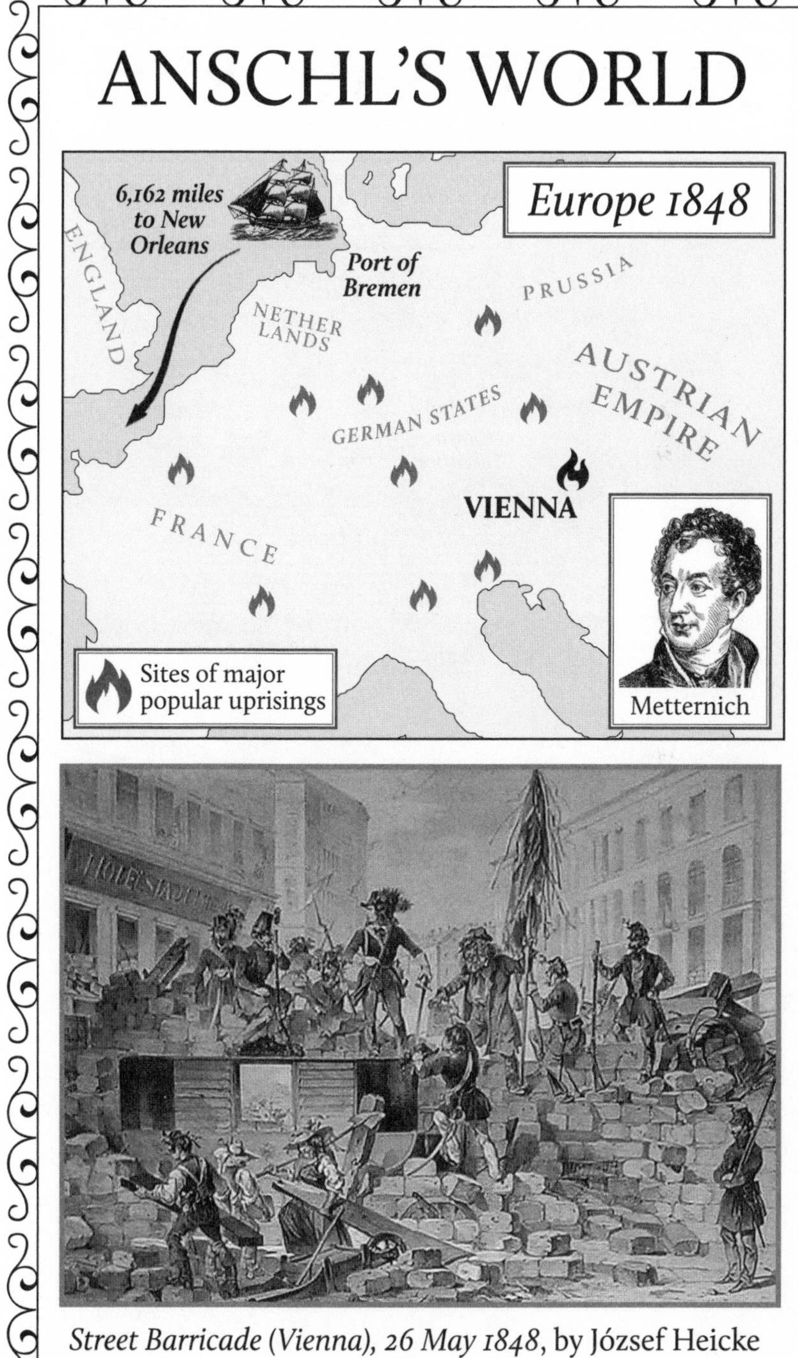

Street Barricade (Vienna), 26 May 1848, by József Heicke

AUGUST'S WORLD

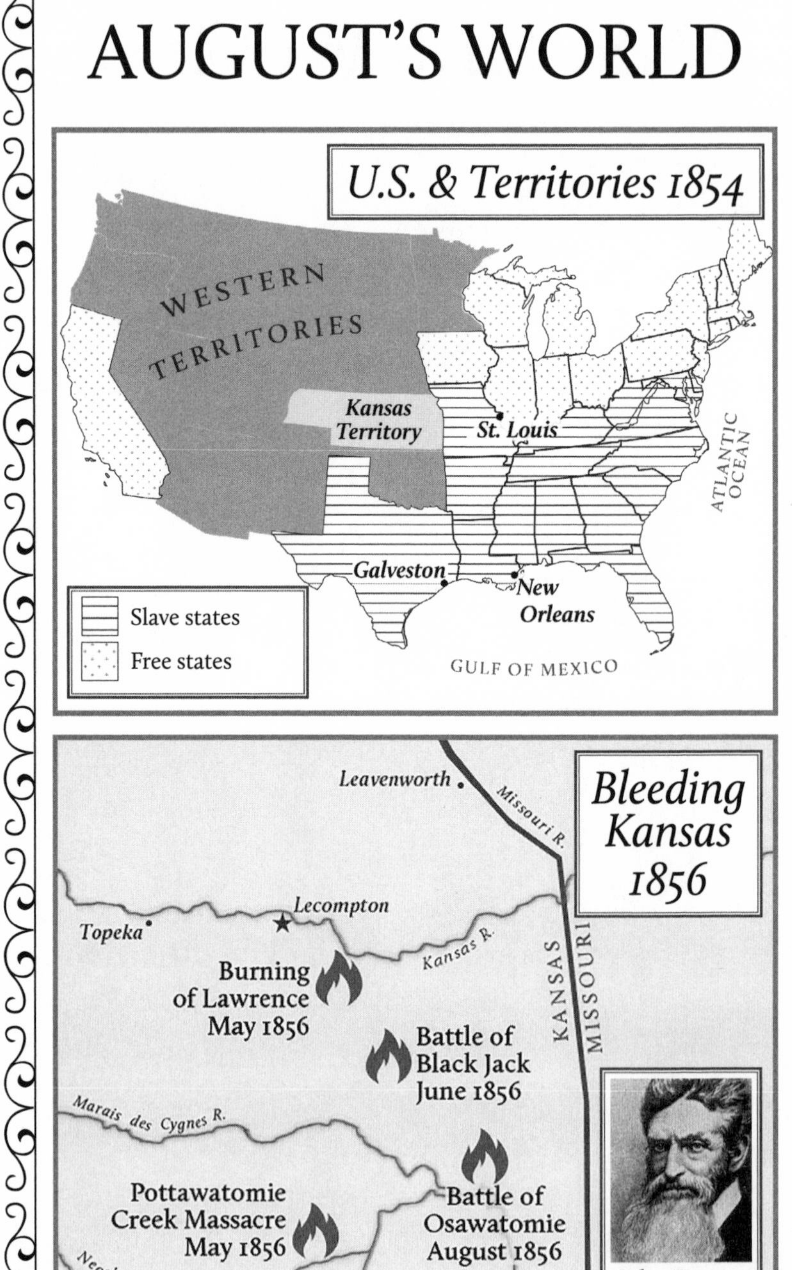

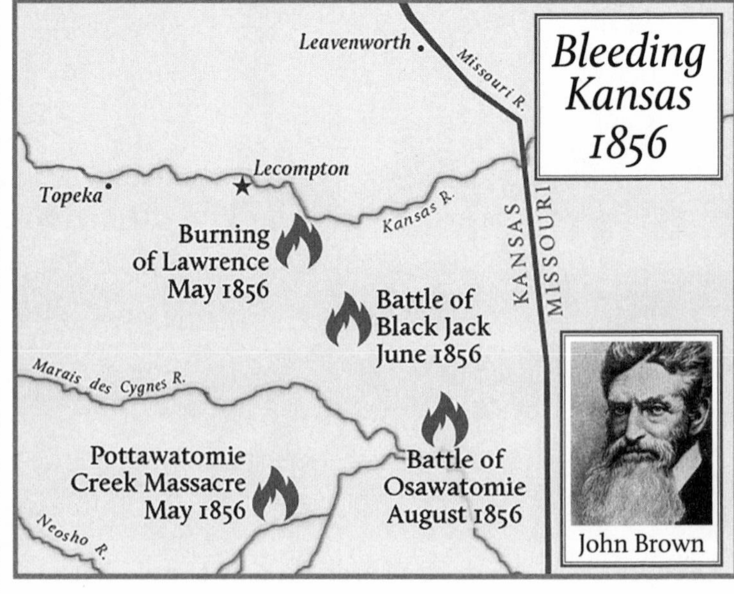

1

ANSCHL

The boy with the long black hair pushed his way through the shouting, jostling mass of students. His school cap was pulled down tight to keep the March wind from blowing it away. His cheeks were flushed, not with cold but with excitement. His thin body seemed to draw energy from the huge crowd, propelling him on toward the front. Finally he reached the steps of Vienna's great stone council hall. He bounded up one step, turned, and looked around.

Where is he?

Suddenly there was a hand on his shoulder.

"Anschl!"

He turned around to see Heinrech Spitzer standing on the step with him. He had a huge grin on his face.

"Can you believe this is happening, Anschl?" Heinrech said.

"*What* is happening? I just got here."

"Well, so far, nothing. But look around! Have you ever seen Council Square like this?"

In front of them were hundreds of students. They were squeezed in tight toward the front. The air buzzed with their chatter.

Solitary cries began to ring out across the square.

"Give us an answer!"

"We demand a Constitution!"

"Metternich must go!"

The yelling startled Anschl. He looked around nervously.

"Don't be frightened," Heinrech said. "Every few minutes someone yells out a slogan, and it gives the others some courage. So then *they* start yelling, and when that's out of their system, they stop." He smirked. "I think they're just doing it to keep warm."

I could use some of that courage, Anschl thought. "But what about the spies?"

Heinrech made a sweeping gesture across the square with one arm.

"Look at all these people!" he said. "What's a spy going to do — go back and tell Prince Metternich that *a thousand people* said bad things about him?"

He laughed. Anschl forced a smile.

They had grown up as constant companions in the

Jewish section of Vienna. Heinrech, one year older, was a little shorter than his friend and about twice as wide. He was also the most good-natured person Anschl Bondi had ever met. When Anschl needed his spirits lifted, he knew where to turn. He almost didn't come to the protest, but Heinrech talked him into it.

"Everyone is going. People want to say that they were at the first protest rally. Who knows? You might be able to tell your grandchildren about it someday. 'Yes, my little ones, I was there at the very moment that the *ancien regime* collapsed.'

"Besides," Heinrech added, "we'll be making so much noise you won't be able to study anyway."

All that winter, a group of students at the academy had been meeting secretly to talk about revolution. Heinrech had been invited first. He vouched for Anschl. Mostly, the group got together to debate topics like which was better, a violent revolution or a nonviolent one. It was a debate club, really. Nobody in the group was plotting to overthrow the government. But everyone knew what they were doing was dangerous. Prince Metternich had declared all such meetings to be illegal. And Anschl had been taught from an early age to fear Metternich.

"Do not so much as utter his name," his mother had warned him. "He has spies *everywhere.*"

"Including the academy, Mother?" he asked.

"Of course he has spies in the academy. Your classmates go home and talk about their day with their parents. Do you think they don't get asked what their Jewish friends are saying about the prince?"

So when Heinrech invited him to join the secret group at school, Anschl decided not to tell his mother. There was already one Bondi in jail. The thought of her Anschl going to illegal meetings would have her worrying day and night about him — if she wasn't already.

Chants were now ringing nonstop throughout the square. Students kept filing in from the narrow streets. Anschl felt the crowd growing restless. The boys passed the time trying to guess the attendance.

"According to my calculations, the capacity of Council Square is two thousand persons," Anschl said.

"Shaped like you or like me?" Heinrech said. "If they're my size, fifteen hundred, tops."

They looked out at the solid mass of humanity.

Amazing, Anschl thought. *From our little group to a revolution, just like that.*

It had all happened so quickly. One morning he walked into his mathematics class and found several boys talking excitedly.

"Anschl," one called out, "what do you think about the news from Paris?"

"There's news from Paris?"

"King Louis Phillippe abdicated his throne! And it was because of a student protest!"

The others filled in the details. The French king had sent his army to arrest the students. But the soldiers were stopped by ten-foot-high barricades the students had built out of cobblestones torn from the streets. The king was outraged. He ordered his troops to start shooting the protesters. They refused. And that was the end of Louis Phillippe.

Anschl was speechless — and not just at the news from Paris. Until that moment, no one in his math class had shown the slightest interest in world affairs.

By the end of the day it seemed the whole school knew what had happened to the French king. From there the student protest took on a life of its own. It seemed to organize itself. Word got around that every school in Vienna would be represented at Council Square.

And so they are, thought Anschl. *Everyone is here!* He began to count all the different school uniforms and caps in the crowd.

Suddenly, he heard the beating of drums in the distance.

"Sounds like they brought the band with them," Heinrech said. He meant it as a joke, but Anschl noticed he wasn't smiling anymore.

The drumbeat grew louder and louder until it became deafening. At that moment a battalion of soldiers appeared. They marched into the square and came to a stop not twenty feet from the boys. The students in front of them were forced back, squeezing in tightly around Anschl and Heinrech.

The soldiers stood at attention in a line. He studied

the soldier's bayonets, noticing how they glistened at the end of their muskets.

"They must spend all day polishing those things," he whispered in Heinrech's ear. Heinrech just nodded.

The crowd was silent. Then, far behind him, Anschl heard someone yell: "Constitution!"

Someone else followed that with, "We demand an answer!"

Just then, a ferocious-looking man in a plumed helmet marched in front of the battalion. Anschl felt a chill on the back of his neck. The commander drew his saber and brandished it at the students.

"Do you want your answer?" he shouted. "Here it is, you pack of dogs! Clear the square!"

Anschl scanned the eyes of the soldiers. *Not Viennese,* he thought. *Probably mercenaries. Brought in just to deal with us.*

The commander's face was hot with anger, his eyes blazing with hate. Anschl had never seen a face like his before.

"I order you back!" he shouted. "Go back or we fire!" But nobody moved.

Can't he see we're squeezed in here? he thought. *Nobody could move if they wanted to.*

The commander turned his back to Anschl.

"Take aim!" he ordered his men, and stepped aside.

Anschl heard the click of the flintlocks. He and the students in front were looking down the barrels of twenty muskets.

His brain screamed.

They — wouldn't — DARE!

The commander raised his saber.

"Fire!"

The crash of musketry nearly split Anschl's ears. Heinrech fell. Another student dropped, then another. Anschl was dragged down with them.

Lying stunned on the cobblestones, he heard the commander's crazed voice again.

"Fix bayonets! Charge!"

The drums beat wildly, the bugles blew the piercing notes of the attack. Anschl heard the heavy boots of the advancing soldiers. Desperately he tried to raise himself. Before he could move, he felt a bayonet rip into his back. Another soldier struck him on the head and shoulders with a musket butt.

Amid the clouds of smoke hanging over the square, the students struggled against the battalion. As he writhed on the ground, Anschl could hear the screams of the wounded above the rattle of musket fire.

The attack passed over them. Barely aware of his own pain, he yelled for help. Another student came over and the two dragged Heinrech, who was unresponsive, away from the chaos.

They found a side street where they could rest their fallen comrade against a doorstep. Anschl ripped open Heinrech's shirt and saw a gruesome entry wound. At that moment the insanity around him seemed to fall away. Everything was calm again.

He's dead.

A moment later Anschl heard a musket shot in the distance and came to his senses. The other boy had run off. He looked down. His clothes were torn. His face throbbed with pain. He put a hand to his cheek and it stung. When he looked at his hand, there was blood.

Still in shock, Anschl took off his overcoat and draped it over Heinrech's body.

"I'll come back for you," he told the lifeless form.

Then he staggered home.

MARTHA

His mother was there when he came through the door. Martha Bondi gasped.

"Anschl! CHAIA!"

Anschl's sister came running into the room. She screamed.

They helped him to his bed and removed his tattered clothes. Then they began to wash and bandage his wounds. He said nothing as they worked.

Then Chaia asked, "Where is Heinrech?"

He tried to say something, but he began to cry. Martha sat down and took him in her arms. Chaia brought him hot tea and medicine.

That night, Anschl dreamed he was running through the streets of Vienna ... running ... running ... looking for

Heinrech. He had left his body somewhere. But where? There were so many side streets off Council Square, more than he remembered there being.

Where are you, Heinrech?

He turned one corner and saw a group of students with clubs. They were being met by squadrons of Hapsburg cavalry. Sparks flew from the horses' hoofs. The heavy sabers of their riders slashed at the boys on the ground. Anschl heard a musket explode, then saw a horse rear up and throw its rider. He kept running.

HEINRECH!

He spent hours looking.

When he finally awoke, it was mid-afternoon of the next day. There was shouting in the street. His head ached and he could barely move his arms. The noise outside grew louder. He pulled himself out of bed and went to the window. Below he could see students racing toward the university. A bell clanged in one of the towers.

He stood up, took a few minutes to steady himself, then dressed. He dashed out of his room and — before Martha could object — was out the door.

As he approached University Square, he started to pick up fragments of the news. "Metternich is gone!" said one. "The emperor agrees to our demands!" said another. He walked faster.

Was this it? The end of the monarchy?

But when he arrived at school, he found dozens of boys standing in line. They were being issued rifles and ammunition. A Catholic priest appeared before him. The priest's eyes were serious, full of grim purpose.

"We meet here tomorrow morning for drills," the priest said to Anschl.

When he returned home, his mother was waiting.

"Why did you run out? You should be in bed!" she cried.

Then she saw the gun in his hand. "What is this?"

"The students are forming their own militia," he said. "We will be called the Academic Legion. Father Fuester will be our commandant."

"Anschl!" she said. There was terror in her voice. "You will be killed! *Then* what will I do?"

Anschl's shoulders slumped. His mother's eyes were welling with tears. He looked away. He knew she would be upset at seeing the gun. So he had practiced a little speech he was going to give when he got home. Now, however, he could not find the words. He started to speak, then stopped. He could hear her crying softly.

He stared at the wall and thought of something to say.

Finally he asked her, "Mother, do you think Father would want me to join the fight for freedom?"

The question was a piercing dagger to heart of Martha Bondi. For they both knew the answer.

Two years ago, the authorities had come for Herz Emmanuel, Anschl's father. He had been sitting in a debtor's prison ever since. After the failure of his trading company, he was left with unpaid bills. In the eyes of the law that made him a common criminal. The judges serving Prince Metternich were corrupt to a man. They all accepted bribes — no, they *insisted* on bribes. Anschl had watched his mother take money from her purse and hand it to the judge overseeing Herz Emmanuel's case. And yet, month after month, the proceedings did not move forward. Further bribes were accepted. Still his father languished in jail.

They bled her dry, Anschl thought. *Wanted to see how much money they could get out of a Jewish family.*

All their clothing, except what they wore on their backs, went to the pawnbroker. Then, piece by piece, the household goods started disappearing. Martha kept only two things of value, the silver wine cup and the menorah, for their religious ceremonies. Everything else was sold. Their nice dishes were replaced by cheap wooden plates and bowls. And every day the Bondis ate the same meals on them: a few cocoa beans boiled in water for breakfast, black bread and potatoes at night. Meanwhile, his father withered away in a prison cell.

If anyone should be praying for the collapse of this rotten government, it should be you, Mother.

When Herz Emmanuel Bondi was a young man, he had been in the medical corps during Napoleon Bonaparte's campaigns. He greatly admired Napoleon. "That man did more to help the Jews than anyone since Maimonides," he told Anschl. "He treated us as equals."

You know what Father would want. He would want me

fighting for freedom.

But Anschl kept his thoughts to himself, and waited on his mother.

After a while her quiet sobbing ceased. Anschl turned to face her. She was still dabbing her eyes with a handkerchief. Then she collected herself and looked bravely into the eyes of her only son.

"May God keep you from harm," Martha Bondi said.

BARRICADES

Overnight Vienna turned into a city at war. Wherever Anschl went, he saw men and boys marching in formation and taking target practice. Two main militias had sprung up: the National Guard for the adults, and the Academic Legion for the students. Every afternoon Anschl and his comrades reported to University Square. After their drills they sat drinking beer and discussing the latest news and gossip. It was the highlight of his day. He and everyone else had lost interest in their studies. School officials moved up the date for final examinations, just to get them over with.

Two months after the first attack, Anschl heard alarm bells ringing from University Square. He seized his musket and hurried over. The square was already filled with students. He went up to an older cadet named Thomas.

"What's the news?"

"Metternich is sending in all he's got," Thomas replied, looking off in the distance.

"What does *that* mean?"

"At least twenty thousand men. The scouts say they've hauled in cannon as well."

Anschl absorbed that number. *Metternich must have gathered up every mercenary in Europe.*

"So what are we doing?" he asked.

"Did you hear me?" Thomas cried. "Vienna does not even have ten thousand people prepared to defend it!"

Anschl looked at the others. They were all standing around talking, waiting nervously for orders.

"So ... we just let them advance on us? Like last time?"

The older cadet whipped his head around at Anschl. "Do you have any better ideas?" he barked.

I might, Anschl thought as he walked away.

He started thinking back to the day Heinrech was killed. *The mercenaries didn't care about us. They just shot their way through. How do we keep them from doing that again?*

He walked along the cobblestones, pondering this question. Suddenly, he stopped. He looked down. At the cobblestones.

Barricades!

He ran over to the nearest group of students.

"Why can't we build barricades?" he asked them. "Like

the students in Paris did?"

"Barricades? With what?" someone said.

Anschl pointed straight down.

"*Those*?" another said in disbelief.

"Stay where you are," said Anschl, and he hurried away.

Coming to the first house at the edge of the square, he knocked on the door. An old lady appeared.

"Pardon, ma'am," he said. "I'm in need of some tools."

Moments later he appeared back at the center of the square holding a pick, a hammer, and a crowbar.

"Watch this," Anschl said. He dropped to his knees and began pounding the pick between two cobblestones. Within a few moments he had the crowbar under one of the stones. He gave it a hard push and the stone came loose. Another push and a corner came up. He wedged it upward with both hands until it was completely free.

"See?" he said. "Now if we can just ..."

He looked up. Everyone was gone.

Within minutes there were dozens of students prying up the cobblestones of University Square. As each stone was loosened, it was hauled to the entrance of the square. Others dragged in furniture, cabinets — anything heavy that could be stacked — and in less than an hour the first barricade was raised.

By now Anschl's arms were aching, his hands torn by the rough paving blocks. He climbed atop the barricade to keep a lookout.

"Hey Anschl!"

burned out. The priest's face was pale and drawn. He showed no emotion as he listened to Anschl's report.

"Good," he finally said. "If we hadn't been ready they'd have shot us down in the streets. Perhaps we'll sleep in our beds tonight."

Perhaps we'll sleep tonight? This was not the response Anschl had expected. He wasn't even feeling tired! The students had fought back. The whole city was barricaded by now. Metternich had lost. It was time to demand freedom for the people of Vienna. It was time to join with the people of Prague, and Paris, and Milan, and Budapest, and Dresden, in demanding freedom from tyrants. *Now!*

But the priest simply said, "You are dismissed," and went back to staring at the papers on his table.

Disappointed, Anschl turned to leave. He was almost to the door when he heard Father Fuester ask, "Aren't you the boy who started the first barricade last night?"

Anschl turned to face the priest, who had not taken his gaze off his papers.

"Yes," Anschl said.

Father Fuester looked up at the boy. His eyes were still serious, but he had a sad smile on his face. Anschl thought he looked very tired.

"You must know how fitting it is for a Jew to raise the first barricade," the priest said.

Anschl walked home thinking about what Father Fuester had said. He thought about all the times growing up when his father had regaled him with stories of the

It was Moritz, seated atop the wall a few feet away. pointed off in the distance. Anschl looked — and couldı believe what he was seeing. Another barricade was goir up a half mile away!

"Word spreads fast," Moritz said.

An hour later, Anschl started to hear the rattle of artillery and the tramp of boots. Looking over the wall, he saw a detachment of grenadiers come into sight. Other students climbed up the barricade. They all leveled their muskets, ready for the attack.

The grenadiers approached the barricade. But before they got very close, they stopped.

"What are they doing?" someone below called out.

"Not a thing," Anschl said, keeping his gaze on the grenadiers. "It seems a barricade of stone did not figure in their plans."

A student fixed the banner of the Academic Legion to a pole and raised it over the barricade for the prince's troops to see. But the grenadiers kept their distance. Not a single shot was fired during the night.

Toward daybreak, a messenger from the National Guard approached the barricade.

"Truce!" he cried. "The emperor declares a truce!"

Anschl scrambled down the wall. He could hardly wait to share the news with his commandant.

Running into the school building, he burst inside to find Father Fuester standing over a table covered with maps and papers. The candles on the table had nearly great Jewish warriors. Men like Judas Maccabeus and Simon Bar-Kokhba who had led popular revolts against the tyrants of their day. How inspired he had been by their lives.

To be linked to those great men filled Anschl's heart with pride. But only for a moment. Then a thought came to mind, and sorrow overtook him.

If only Heinrech were here.

HERZ EMMANUEL

Just as Father Fuester had warned, Metternich's armies began bombarding the barricades. The prince had decided on a siege. The priest glumly predicted what was to come: "Innocent civilians will be killed. Stores will close. The people will slowly starve until their resistance crumbles."

If there was a bright side to all this, it was that the courts disbanded, and Herz Emmanuel was released from debtor's prison. Anschl came home from the Academic Legion one night and there he was, eating beef stew. Martha had bought some meat for the occasion.

He stood up to embrace Anschl.

"You are so tall now," he said, clasping the boy by the shoulders. "So much happens when you leave for two years." Suddenly Herz Emmanuel's face looked puzzled.

"Your rifle — where is it?" he asked. "I know all about the Academic Legion."

"I'm leaving it at Moritz's house."

"I told him I do not want it in here," Martha added.

She ladled out a bowl of stew for Anschl, and he joined them at the table.

"While I was in prison, I heard a great deal about Metternich's strategy from my guards. They were moving their families out of Vienna. They said the prince is planning a major offensive this fall."

"What kind of offensive?" Anschl asked. "They already have the city surrounded. They lack the strength to push past our barricades."

"Metternich has been distracted," his father said. "He has been putting down rebellions in Prague and Budapest. When those scores are settled, he will bring an army to Vienna that will make these twenty thousand seem like a small force."

Anschl stopped eating. "What are you saying, Father?"

"I'm saying, dear Anschl, that as Jews we must think not only about the struggle, we must think about our survival."

"Are you saying you think we will be crushed?" Anschl's voice was rising.

"Anschl!" Martha said sternly. "Listen to your Father."

"All I am saying is that the prospects for victory here are not so good," Herz Emmanuel said. "We need to think about going somewhere else. I cannot do business in a city that is under siege. How do you expect us to survive as a family if we cannot afford food or rent?"

Anschl ate the rest of his meal in sulky silence.

That night, while everyone slept, he lay in bed with the covers thrown off. His whole body was on fire.

How could he ask this of me? I was defending freedom while he was gone! If Metternich was still in Vienna, he would still be in that jail cell. Does he not know this? He's asking me to abandon the struggle. Where is your Simon Bar-Kokhba now, Father? Where is that inspiring story about Judas Maccabeus? Maybe I need to tell it to you, since your memory is slipping...

But it was no use. He could never speak that way to his parents.

In fact, Anschl barely spoke to his father for weeks. He would come home from the Academic Legion and see Herz Emmanuel hunched over the family table with an ink quill and paper, writing letters. He walked by, pretending to be not the slightest bit curious.

Coming home from his drills one evening, Anschl found his father waiting for him.

"We are going to America," Herz Emmanuel said.

Anschl was stunned.

"I have tried everything, my son. But there is no work

for me here or anywhere else in Austria."

America?!

He had guessed correctly. His father had been writing friends and relatives for help. What he hadn't guessed was that he was sending letters halfway around the world.

"When?" he asked.

"The next boat leaves Bremen on the twenty-third," Herz Emmanuel said.

THE REBECCA

Anschl was leaning forward on the rail of the *Rebecca*. He was leaning about as far forward as a passenger dared to lean. It was the position you might assume if you were seasick. But Anschl wasn't seasick. He was, however, sick of the sea. Sick of looking at it. Sick of being on it.

The fact that he could see land somehow only made things worse. The *Rebecca* had spent three weeks sailing across the Atlantic. Three weeks of endless ocean, endless sky, endless boredom. Then one morning, Anschl woke up early, went out on deck, and saw shoreline. He rushed into the berth where his father was still sleeping.

"I see land!" he cried.

Herz Emmanuel turned over and slowly opened his

eyes to look at Anschl.

"Land, Father, land!"

His father regarded him wearily.

"If you see land, it means we have two more weeks at sea."

"Two more *weeks?!?*"

"Yes, my son. You saw Nova Scotia."

At breakfast, the captain offered to bring Anschl into the great cabin to look at his map. The captain pointed to Nova Scotia, right in the center. Anschl's heart sank.

We're closer to Ireland than New Orleans!

Since then, he had watched gloomily as the *Rebecca* bumped along the Eastern seaboard, tormenting him with the occasional glimpse of the mainland. One afternoon he spent hours hatching an elaborate plot in his head. While no one was looking, he would lower himself in one of the *Rebecca's* small boats and paddle for shore.

If I did it at night, I could reach land before anyone noticed I was missing. Of course, they'd probably miss the boat before they missed me.

It wasn't a very serious plan. But just thinking about it somehow made the day go by faster.

Besides, even if my plan worked flawlessly, I would still *be in America.*

Anschl had been in a deep funk ever since the train had pulled out of the station in Vienna. Bitter tears had flowed as the last familiar sight — the cross atop St. Stephen's church — disappeared from view. He had left his whole life behind: his friends, the Academic Legion, and the cause of freedom they had pledged their lives to.

The night before his departure, he had stayed out with his closest friends, boys he had grown up with in the Jewish quarter. They had all told him the same thing: Go. Obey your parents. It may not end well here. Providence is throwing you a lifeline. Take it.

Father had done his best to make the long trip enjoyable. With money given to him by relatives, he reserved a cabin on the upper deck of the boat. The family shared a small sitting room during the day, then retired to separate sleeping berths. They ate meals prepared by the crew. It was hardly the lap of luxury, but their relatives didn't want the Bondis to ride in steerage.

He had also brought reading material for himself and Anschl: newspapers, journals, books. "I thought this would especially interest you," Herz Emmanuel said. He handed Anschl a thin volume in German. "Straight from the printer in London."

The Communist Manifesto. Anschl knew all about it. Word about Karl Marx's controversial book had traveled across Europe faster than the book itself.

"Thank you," he said. "I'll read it."

"And then maybe we can discuss Marx's theory."

Anschl nodded. He had heard enough about it to know that Marx had divided the world into two groups of people: the working class and the upper class.

And did you notice, Father, that we are staying in the up-

per deck cabins?

Anschl knew his father was trying to connect with him. But Marxist theory didn't do anyone a whole lot of good on a sailing ship. And he failed to see how it was going to do him much good in America, either.

If anyone in America even reads books in German.

A thought occurred to him.

Wait — does this mean I have to learn English?

As it was hurricane season, the *Rebecca* ran into its share of blustery winds and drenching rain. Anschl welcomed the stormy weather, for two reasons: it broke the grinding monotony of a typical day, and it made his father seasick. He felt a little guilty knowing he was enjoying his father's misery ... but *just* a little.

When the seas were calm, Anschl went down to the main deck to see if any passengers had come up from steerage for fresh air. He met a rabbi from Poland who was fleeing violence at home. He traded war stories with young radicals who had been wanted by police in Hungary and Germany. Mostly, though, he met a lot of men who reminded him of his father.

"Where I am from, no work," a man named Peter told him one day. Peter was from Russia. His wife and five children were below. He just stared off into the distance, puffing on a cigar, even when talking with Anschl. He looked sad.

"I work like Siberian sled-dog if only someone gives me chance," Peter said.

One day a boy Anschl's age came up on deck. He introduced himself as Stephen, from Hungary. His clothes were tattered and dirty, and he looked like he hadn't had a good night's sleep in months. But as soon as he found out where Anschl was from, he perked up.

"Your revolution started *our* revolution!" Stephen said. "I was in Buda when we learned about the uprising in Vienna. That made the radicals very happy. And it made the officials very nervous. Things started to change quickly after that."

Anschl had never been down to the steerage section, so he asked his new friend to take him there.

They climbed down into the darkness. Anschl stood at the bottom of the ladder for a few moments, squinting blindly. When his eyes finally adjusted to the darkness, he was amazed at what he saw. Two hundred immigrants were living side by side. For five weeks they had been shoehorned into little more than a crawl space between the main deck and the cargo hold. There were hard wooden bunks everywhere.

Anschl saw several families eating together. *Is that soup? How do they even cook down here?*

He found Stephen sitting on a trunk with hand lettering on it. The lettering said ISTVAN POKORNY. Two girls were sitting on the bed knitting.

"These are my sisters," he said, "and that's my mother, helping Katazina with her baby." Anschl looked behind him and saw a young woman was changing the diaper on a tiny baby. Two older women were making faces at the baby to keep it amused.

"That baby looks like it was just born," Anschl said.

"He *was* just born," Stephen said. "About a week ago they delivered him. And we have another woman expecting over there. If we don't reach New Orleans soon, we're going to have another delivery at sea."

"How do you know Katazina?"

"We met on the ship. She's from Poland. Her husband and my dad are off somewhere smoking and arguing. Probably about philosophy."

Anschl pointed at the chest. "Is that your father's name, Istvan?"

"This is *my* trunk," he said. "Istvan is Hungarian for Stephen. My father said if you don't make your name easy for Americans to spell, they'll spell it however they feel like spelling it. So when we boarded the ship, he wrote down my name as Stephen."

That night, Anschl lay awake in his berth, unable to sleep. He listened to the night winds howling and the sails flapping. He kept thinking about what he had seen that day in steerage.

These humble immigrants, too poor to afford a cabin, had formed into a little community. Just like that. They had probably spent their whole lives in one place. They had known the same people, gone to the same schools, and buried their elders in the same churchyards for centuries. Then, suddenly, they had been driven out by the king's army or an anti-Jewish mob. Or maybe they were just tired of being poor and hungry. Whatever happened, they were here now, sharing their food, their sleeping quarters, their stories, with complete strangers.

And then they were going to arrive in America. They would scatter to the four corners of the continent. They would find someplace to live. Their neighbors would be complete strangers, probably other hard-working immigrants like themselves. And they would build another community from scratch.

Just like I'll have to do.

One day, Herz Emmanuel and his son were out on the main deck, talking about their new home.

"In America," his father said, "no one fears the prince or the army. The army serves the *people*. The *people* decide who will lead them. The elections are free and fair. And another thing. There will be no more insults of our people or our faith. The Constitution has separated the church and the government. We have the freedom to practice our religion as we please. America is the land of liberty."

Anschl just stared off at sea. Nothing his father said

was new to him. He and his comrades in the Academic Legion had discussed and debated all of the major nations of the world — France, America, England, Russia — and he knew none of them was a perfect place to live.

"Father," said Anschl. He turned and tried to look as innocent as possible. "I have heard that the United States Constitution allows slavery. Is that true?"

Herz Emmanuel frowned. "Of course it does, Anschl. You know that."

"But you say it is the land of liberty. How can that be, when a man is able to make another man his slave?"

Now it was the father's turn to be irritated.

"Perhaps we should wait until we are there before passing judgment on our new country," he said sharply, then walked off.

Anschl was toying with his father, and that was a cruel thing to do. He knew that. He knew he should feel bad for doing it. But he didn't. For once on this trip, he felt fully alive.

AUGUST

One morning Anschl heard a familiar voice call out, "Land!" It was the captain.

He stepped out of his cabin and saw that everyone in steerage had come up the ladders and was crowding the main deck. They were pointing in the distance and shouting excitedly in several languages.

"Look, ships!"

"And houses!"

Anschl was expecting to take in a splendid view of the New Orleans waterfront. Instead, all he saw was a swamp with a few sad-looking buildings thrown up near the shore.

"Don't get too excited, folks," the captain said. "This is Balize, a pretty little town where we're going to drop anchor. Tomorrow a tugboat is going to come over and tow us into New Orleans.

"Now folks," he continued, "they've got some real nice eating and drinking establishments here, so if you've forgotten what the feel of *terra firma* is like, or just want to experience some of the Southern hospitality here, why, you're welcome to go ashore tonight."

Anschl turned to his father. "What did he say?"

"He said we should be in New Orleans in another day or two," said Herz Emmanuel.

Another day or two!?!? Anschl couldn't believe it. *When is this trip going to end?!?*

He went to his sleeping berth and pulled the covers over his head.

The next morning he awoke to the smell of something burning.

He ran outside. He was expecting to see the ship on fire. But there was no smoke. It was very quiet above deck. He looked to his east. The full yolk of the sun had just cleared the horizon. It was early.

He turned around. The *Rebecca* was tied to a dock, and a gangplank led down to shore.

He smelled smoke again. It had a funny odor. *That's not wood smoke,* he thought. *Someone's burning their crops.*

He looked past the sad-looking houses and establishments. Then he saw it, down a road that led out of town. A large building with black wispy smoke coming out of it.

I suppose it's time to explore this new country of mine.

As he approached the building, he spotted two black men hauling wood. At first they appeared to be wearing tunics, like actors in a Shakespearean play. As he got closer, however, Anschl realized the men were wearing coffee sacks. The sack was cut open at both ends, then slipped on and tied at the waist with string.

Don't they have their own clothing? Did they just step off the slave ship and come right here?

He felt a knot in his stomach, but he had to know more. He followed the men into the building.

It was a large, open room. Anschl figured it was at least a hundred fifty feet long and thirty feet high. The smell was overpowering. So was the heat and humidity.

I can't imagine what it's like here in the afternoon.

Next to him was a large and noisy boiler. The two men in sacks started feeding wood into the boiler's firebox. Filling the center of the room was an enormous contraption the size of a small house. At one end of the machine was a large gear wheel. It powered two huge rollers.

What is this — the world's largest laundry wringer?

Several more dark-skinned, coffee-sack-wearing workers appeared, hauling wagon loads of green, woody stalks. They stopped at the other end of the contraption and started unloading the stalks onto a conveyor belt.

He watched the stalks as they disappeared between the

two rollers. Over the din of the boiler, he could hear crunching sounds as the stalks were smashed by the rollers.

Suddenly a voice behind him boomed out, "We usually don't do tours this early!"

Anschl almost jumped out of his boots. He turned around to see a friendly-looking older white man. He had a lit cigar in one hand. He was the only person in the building wearing regular work clothes.

The man chuckled. "Didn't mean to scare you!" he said in a loud voice. "Say now, you best keep yo' distance from this machine! It's the sugar cane harvest and these nig'rahs got work to do! They'll run you right over! They gotta daily quota to meet, and we set it high! We got to! We want you city folks to always have the finest, purest, whitest sugar on yo' breakfast table!"

Anschl nodded.

"Where you from, boy?"

Anschl knew enough English to answer the question.

"*Wien*, sir."

"Vee-yun? I ain't heard of that town. Well, as I say, we ain't got anyone to show you 'round right now, but yo' welcome to stand there and observe."

Anschl nodded.

A crashing sound came from the far end of the room. Anschl whirled around and saw that a wagon had tipped over. One of the workers was trapped under it. It looked like his leg was pinned beneath a wheel.

Immediately the white man strode away toward the accident, barking over the noise. "Hey! Git that wagon up! We're losin' time!" The workers looked up and saw the white man approaching. Anschl noticed that their body language instantly changed. Everyone scurried behind the wagon and began pushing. After a few heaves they got it up on its wheels. Then the whole wagon train slowly moved away. The workers pulled the wagon toward an open door on the building's far end. The white man trailed behind, barking orders.

As Anschl watched the parade of people leaving, something out of the corner of his eye moved. He looked back at the accident scene and noticed ... a coffee sack.

The injured worker. They left him behind.

He was writhing on the ground in obvious pain. Anschl looked at him in disbelief.

Suddenly his senses all began to overload. He was sweating profusely, the steam engine sounded incredibly loud, and whatever was burning now smelled so awful, he felt he might vomit.

Must — get out — NOW.

He sprinted down the road and back to the boat.

"It sounds as though you walked into a sugar mill," Herz Emmanuel said over breakfast. "They probably run all day and night during the harvest season."

"I've heard they give tours to the public," said Mr. Volz, an older gentleman from the other cabin. All the cabin guests ate together. Everyone had listened with great interest as Anschl described what he had seen.

"I wonder if there is time to go on a tour before our ship is pulled to New Orleans," Mr. Volz continued. "I think it would be most enlightening."

"It wasn't enlightening at all," Anschl shot back. "It was the most disgusting thing I'd seen in my life."

"Anschl!" his mother scolded him. But he was too furious to stop.

"Human beings dressed in sacks, working in those conditions! And I could just tell, the *minute* I left the building, that supervisor would be getting out his whip. He would *beat* those people for wasting his precious time!"

Mr. Volz was momentarily speechless. Anschl got up and left the cabin.

Later, Herz Emmanuel came out to find him. He was staring at the sugar mill. The two watched it smoke for a while.

"I hope you don't mind if I begin judging my new country *now*, Father," Anschl said.

"Be my guest," said Herz Emmanuel quietly.

"Also, I've decided to change my name to August."

"But your name is already August, my son."

"That's not what I mean. I want to be called August from now on. Anschl ..."

He swallowed. Tears filled his eyes.

"Anschl is back in Vienna. He's manning the barricades. He's with his comrades, defending freedom. I *loved* Anschl. I loved his *life*, Father. But now I'm here. I can't be Anschl any longer. America is a place where people come to work. They don't come here to be free. They come here to make money. From what I saw this morning, if it comes down to money and freedom, money wins."

"Anschl ..."

"Father, what do you think those African slaves would say about Marx's theory of the working class? Even if they could read German, they're not going to be rising up anytime soon."

Nothing was said for a while.

"I wish Heinrech were here to see this," August said quietly.

"You've been thinking of Heinrech."

"I think of Heinrech every day."

Herz Emmanuel looked over at his son. Tears had run down his cheeks.

"I remember one day when we were having one of our secret meetings," August said. "Heinrech was debating American slavery with Moritz. And Moritz was saying, 'Of course slavery is a terrible thing. But if the African slaves were given their freedom tomorrow, there is no way they could survive on their own. They should be free someday, don't get me wrong! But until they learn how to live as free people, they are probably better off in slavery.' Moritz said he had read reports of plantation owners who were very good to their slaves, and so on.

"When Heinrech heard all this, he laughed. And he said, 'Moritz, do you even *know* how much you sound like Metternich right now? That's what *he* thinks about *us*! He thinks we're too stupid to decide what's best for ourselves. That's *his* job. He was born to it. He had all the best breeding, went to all the best schools, and was taught how to keep an entire people subjugated.'

"And then he said, 'Now that I think about it, Moritz, there was one good slave owner in the Bible. He made sure his subjects were well-fed and clothed and had shelter. In fact, his subjects loved him so much they hated to be away from him.' And Moritz said, 'Really? I don't remember reading that story. Who was this slave owner?'

"And Heinrech just looked at him like he was a complete moron. *'It was PHARAOH!'* he said. And everybody laughed and howled and razzed Moritz about taking the side of the slave owners. Even Moritz had to admit that Heinrech had it all over him that day."

August smiled, thinking about the memory.

"Heinrech was a very clever boy," Herz Emmanuel said. "A very good boy."

They heard a little ship whistle in the distance. They looked to the west. The tugboat was approaching.

"My son, I am sorry I could not find an opportunity back home. Believe me, I tried everything. But there is chaos all over Europe. I lost my business because my trading partners in Italy and Spain went bankrupt. They couldn't pay their bills, so I couldn't pay mine." He sighed. "America just seemed like the best option for all of us."

"I understand, *Pater,*" said August.

They watched the captain descend the gangplank. The tugboat chugged into the port.

"Actually," he added, "the other reason I'm changing my name to August is because it's a word the Americans know how to spell."

Herz Emmanuel nodded sagely.

"I have always been proud of you, my son, never more than I am now," he said. "Our friends in St. Louis tell me that America will be very hard for us at first. We must learn the language and get accustomed to their ways here. But there will be opportunities for you. And I hope someday that Anschl is also able to join us here."

August and his father spent the next hour watching the tugboat as it sidled up to the hull of the *Rebecca* and hitched itself to the big ship.

7

SAINT LOUIS

In New Orleans the Bondis boarded a river boat and crawled seven hundred miles up the Mississippi. Two weeks later — at last — their travels were at an end. Friends from the old country were there to greet them at the dock in St. Louis. They helped the family find a small house for rent and get settled.

And then everyone got to work.

"Prosperity will not magically rain down on us in America," Father had said. However, some epic thunderstorms did. August had never heard such an ear-splitting, wall-shaking sound as Missouri thunder. Water ran into their house from all directions. Herz Emmanuel learned not to keep his papers on the floor after that.

Until the Bondis could learn passable English, their

business prospects were limited. August's mother and sister tried to teach needlework classes, but most German immigrant women were already good with a needle. Herz Emmanuel sold things out of a street cart, but English speakers avoided him.

The best August could do was a job in a store that catered to immigrants. On his first day of work, the shopkeeper walked him to the back of the store and handed him an apron. The shopkeeper waited as August tried to put it on.

The apron strings tied in the back. As he reached around, it dawned on him that he had never tied something this way. He tried looping one string through the other, but he couldn't see what he was doing. He fumbled blindly with the strings for what seemed like forever. He started to sweat. The shopkeeper just stood there, expressionless, refusing to help.

He probably thinks I can't do anything.

Finally the man grabbed August by the shoulder and turned him around. He took the apron strings and brusquely tied them in a knot, then walked away. August stood there, feeling totally humiliated.

He heard footsteps approaching, and turned around. It was the shopkeeper holding a broom. He thrust it into August's hands. August looked down at it.

"What's the matter — don't you know what a broom's for?" the shopkeeper said.

It was the final insult. A storm was welling up inside

August. It had been gathering since that day when his father had told him they were leaving for the New World. All the frustration and hurt he felt, all the goodbyes he'd had to say. They kept piling up like gray clouds. Finally, inside this general store in St. Louis, the storm broke.

His whole body began to shake. Hot, heavy tears started to pour out. He tried to grab part of his apron to cry into, but the shopkeeper had tied it so tightly he couldn't lift it up to his face. So he just hung his head and cried into his shirt. The shopkeeper walked away.

After the storm had passed, August gave the whole store a good sweeping. *Probably the cleanest it's been in years,* he thought. The shopkeeper was nicer toward him, too.

Store work was very boring, however, and August soon went looking for other work. A printer hired him to set type for several foreign-language newspapers that were sold to immigrants from Europe. It was hard, grimy work, but it helped him learn English.

"Here," the printer said one day. He dropped a newspaper from New Orleans on the desk. "Set this in German."

August looked down at the headline:

DOWNFALL OF VIENNA AFTER SIEGE

His eyes widened. He read the story carefully.

"*From Our European Correspondent.*—After a bloody attack of eight days, the citizens of Vienna surrendered to Prince Windischgratz, commander of the imperial troops.

"The attack commenced with shelling of the university, which continued the next day. By 7 o'clock in the evening, all parts of the city were on fire. A counterattack was waged which was completely defeated by the imperial troops.

"The number of Viennese killed is as high as 1500 persons. Prince Windischgratz has dissolved the National Guard and Academic Legion and ordered hundreds of its members jailed."

August leaned back in his chair. His heart was racing and he felt light-headed.

They're all gone ... the resistance ... dead ...

Later, he tearfully read the newspaper story to the others at the supper table.

"I'm sure your friends were very brave," Herz Emmanuel said. "The great hero Judas Maccabeus died in battle as well. I suppose I should have mentioned that when I told you his story."

"Dear, dear Anschl," said his mother as she took his hand. "I just thank God you are here with us now."

He smiled weakly at her and patted her hand.

But he was thinking: *I wish I had stayed.*

August turned sixteen, then seventeen. The memory of Vienna faded. There was no time to think about the past. He was too busy trying to fit in with his fellow

Americans. He started taking night classes and worked all kinds of jobs: gardener, saloon keeper, substitute teacher.

Finally, he felt ready to leave. One evening after supper, he announced his plans to his parents.

"Where are you going?" asked his mother.

"Have you heard about Commodore Perry's expedition to Japan?"

"Yes. I read about it in the newspaper," said his father. "It sounds very exciting. Just the kind of adventure a young man seeks. You are thinking of enlisting?"

"I am," said August.

"And I suppose you have saved up enough of your earnings to pay your way down to New Orleans?"

"I have."

"Is this a military expedition, like your father took with Napoleon?" said Martha.

"The mission will be a peaceful one, Mother," said August. "Commodore Perry is being sent there to open trade relations with Japan."

"August, you are almost eighteen now," said his father. "We could not stop you even if we wanted to. When I was your age, I too had dreams of freedom. You must have your freedom, too."

"But Anschl," said his mother — she still called him Anschl — "will you make us a promise?"

"Of course, Mother."

"When you are done exercising your freedom, come back home."

"I will, Mother."

"And remember, there are others in this country who are not free. You can do them some good."

August was taken aback by this.

"Y-yes, of course."

"It would be a great honor to the memory of your friends in Vienna."

She smiled warmly. He took her hand.

"Thank you, Mother," he said. "I would like to honor them someday."

THE BRAZOS

Cabins are overrated, August decided. He bought deck passage for his steamboat trip down the Mississippi. That first night, he found a quiet space on the boat's main deck and stretched out under the stars, using his knapsack for a pillow.

Steamboats fascinated him, especially the people on them. There were travelers hauling around enormous carpetbags, gamblers wearing glittering diamond stick-pins, and plenty of young men like himself.

"Goin' to California," a lanky redhead from Illinois told him. "Can't decide if I'm going to be fool mining for gold or a sutler selling mining supplies to other fools. There's money to be made out there, either way."

In New Orleans, August found his way to the recruiting office. A sign on the door read:

> *COMMODORE PERRY expresses his regrets that the quota for enlistments having been received, no further applications for the expedition to JAPAN will be accepted.*

He wasn't surprised. He guessed that Perry had all the men he needed by the time the news reached St. Louis. The truth was, August had wanted desperately to get out of town. The trip to Japan was just a handy excuse. So now he would try the California gold rush instead.

"Sixty dollars."

A fat man with greasy hands was sitting behind a card table in the lobby of a New Orleans hotel. August had been told he was selling direct passage to the California gold fields.

"You get me sixty dollars, I get you to Sutter's Mill in under a month."

"I have thirty dollars."

"Well then, son, I suggest you change yo' travel plans, 'cause ain't nobody in this town can deliver you to Sutter's Mill for under sixty."

I know how he's making his *gold,* August thought.

He walked around the harbor looking for other prospects. A line of immigrants was waiting at the gangplank of a steamboat. They looked like they had just stepped off the boat from Bremen.

That was our family three years ago, he thought.

He studied the big boat. She had fat smokestacks and her pilot house was decorated with fancy woodwork. The paddle boxes, painted red and gold, bore her name — the *Brazos* — inside a brilliant painted sunburst.

He walked over to the boat and started chatting up two teenage boys.

"Where'd you come from?"

"We arrived yesterday from Bremen."

"How many weeks was your journey?"

"Weeks? It was seventeen days."

"He's wrong," said another. "It was eighteen days."

"You took a steamship over?" August said.

"Of course," the first boy said. "Nobody sails from Bremen anymore."

"Where's this boat heading?"

"Galveston, then up the river to Houston."

Texas! That sounded like a plan.

The riverboat's bell began to clang and the immigrants moved forward. He followed them. As he tried to board, however, a sailor put out his hand and stopped him.

"Sorry, mister," he said. "We got a contract to take these Germans to Houston. If you ain't with 'em, you can't come aboard."

"I'm willing to work."

The sailor just shook his head.

Suddenly a voice called out from overhead.

"Hey, greenhorn! *Sprechen sie* the Dutch?"

A tall man had stepped out of the pilot house. He climbed down a ladder to where August was standing. The sailor turned briskly and saluted him. He was a barrel-chested man, with a black mustache and long sideburns. His weatherbeaten face looked dark under his sparkling white cap. He was definitely the man in charge.

"What's going on here?"

"Captain, this boy wants to go to Texas, but he's not part of the group."

The captain gruffly turned to August. But there was a twinkle in his eye.

"Son," the captain said, "I'm under contract to take this party of German settlers to Houston. But I saw you speaking with those Dutchies in their language, didn't I?"

"You did, sir."

"You read and write, too?"

"Yes, sir."

The big man extended his hand.

"Tom Chubb's my name. I'm master of this ship. I like a boy that ain't scared of a little excitement. Tell you what. If your work's good, you can stay on with me. The river trade is a fast life. If you can't pull your own weight, you'd best stay off this boat."

"I'll be fine," August said.

"Then you just got yourself a job as my clerk and interpreter. Stow your gear below and report back to me."

The captain turned and set a foot on the companionway. "All right, cast off there!" he yelled to the rest of the crew. "Cast off!"

Black smoke poured from the stacks, bells clanged, a whistle blew. The steamboat pulled away from the dock. By the time August returned above deck, the *Brazos* was far from shore.

After Chubb unloaded the immigrants at Houston, he swung around and ran the *Brazos* toward the Gulf of Mexico. He and August became fast friends. In the pilot house, he showed the greenhorn how to take a boat through shallow water.

It was hot and calm on the evening that they approached Galveston Bay. Chubb looked sharply at the sky. "There's a norther comin' up fast!" he said to August. Then he leaned into the speaking tube near the wheel. "Stop engines!" he shouted into the tube. He turned the wheel over to the mate. August followed as he ran out on the bridge. "Drop anchor!" Chubb commanded. "Drop anchor if you don't want to get blown halfway to Houston! Look alive!"

The storm was on them within minutes. The crew raced up and down the decks, securing everything that might be washed away. The *Brazos* pitched and rolled, the wind lashed sheets of rain against August's face as he clung to a railing. The deep voice of Captain Chubb sang out orders and the boat's bell rang wildly.

"She's draggin' anchor!" a deck hand shouted.

The *Brazos* gave a shudder and suddenly swung free. The boat spun in circles as the river water washed over the slanting decks.

"Stand by!" Captain Chubb roared. "She's goin' aground!"

August heard a deep cracking sound and was thrown headlong to the deck. The pilot house windows shattered. Clouds of steam swirled in the wind. August picked himself up and saw Chubb grinning at him.

"You all right, greenhorn?" he asked. "I don't aim to lose a clerk on the first trip!"

"You won't lose me that easily," August answered.

They worked all night securing the *Brazos.* August stayed on deck, heaving lines with the rest of the crew, wading in water up to his belt. The storm passed and the dawn came up clear. He saw that the steamboat had been blown onto a sand bar.

Repairing the damage took several days. When the boat was ready for the deep water, the crew loaded into skiffs attached to the boat and rowed with all their strength. August took an oar and pulled until his arms ached. From the pilot house Chubb bellowed down at him. "Put your back into it, greenhorn! We'll make a river man of you yet!" August could tell he was enjoying himself. At last the *Brazos* came free.

Chubb ran her to Galveston and from there up the Trinity River. Along the way August saw alligators sunning themselves on the shore. Keelboats sailed past loaded with bearskins, deerskins, and lumber that looked like it was cut from trees four feet thick.

During the daytime he kept records of loadings and unloadings, of goods bought and sold, and lists of passengers. Chubb and his other mates taught him how to tie sailors' knots. He learned how to swim and dive and stay underwater.

Whenever the *Brazos* laid over at a landing, August went exploring. The wilderness was inhabited by snakes, scorpions, lizards, jackrabbits, and herds of wild cattle. He learned how to care for snakebites, how to stalk animals in open prairie, how to ride, and how to fish. He began to feel as much at home in Texas as anywhere he had lived.

Late one night, a night when it was just too hot for sleeping, he stood by the railing of the upper deck and listened to the slap of the water. The stars hung low in the sky and seemed to touch the bushes along shore. The sun and wind had tanned his face. The muscles of his body had toughened. August cut a handsome figure in his blue uniform, brass buttons, and white cap.

I could handle this life, he thought. *Chubb's been dropping some pretty strong hints lately. Talking about going into business on his own boat. With me as his partner, perhaps.*

August Bondi, riverboatman.

He liked the sound of that.

We could work on the Mississippi. Then I could visit the family whenever we were in St. Louis and come back to Texas anytime I wanted ...

Suddenly Chubb appeared on deck. He had his pocket watch out and an unhappy look on his face.

"Running awful late tonight," he said. "When we get to our next stop we got about ten tons to unload before dawn. We won't get paid 'less we get back on schedule."

"I'll get it done," August said confidently.

As dawn approached, however, cargo was still waiting to come ashore. August and the stevedores were working frantically to get it all unloaded. The sun was beginning to rise. August heard the ship's whistle blow. Then it blew again.

Chubb must think I don't know what time it is.

"Pulling on that thing isn't going to make us go any faster," he yelled up at the pilot house. But his words were drowned out by the whistle. He turned around and yelled at the stevedores, "Pick up the pace!"

All the men started moving just a little faster ... all of them except William, that is. William was one of the stevedores, a older, gangling black man who seemed to have no muscles at all, but could lift and haul with the rest of them for as long as was needed. William always moved at his own steady pace. And this morning, for whatever reason, it irritated August.

"I said, pick up the *pace!*" he yelled at the black stevedore. William said nothing. He just kept walking up the gangplank.

Without thinking, August clenched the rope in his

right hand and snapped it expertly. It cracked like a whip on William's left shoulder.

William stopped. He rubbed his shoulder, then looked up at August. He looked hurt.

"Massa," he said, "you been the only one who never give me a whippin'. I surely thought you was different from the rest."

The words cut August to the quick. He stood speechless for a moment. Then he turned toward the stevedore.

"William, I —" But he was gone.

The *Brazos* was unloaded and back on schedule. August was exhausted from his all-nighter. But he lay in his bunk for hours, unable to sleep, feeling feverish and sick to his stomach.

I never would have done that to William if he was white.

Then he had another thought.

I've become the man in the sugar mill.

Yes, William was a free man. But August, without even thinking, had cracked a whip on him. The more he thought about it, the worse he felt.

Now he was reviewing scenes from the past few months. The times the *Brazos* would pull into a port and the dock was crowded with white, well-to-do people. Always, always, they had slaves in tow — men, women, and children. At first the sight had startled him. Now, he hardly noticed them at all.

And that's just what people want you to do here. They want you to ignore the slaves. Or else admire how proper they act and how nicely they're dressed.

He thought back to the fancy ball he attended. One of the regular passengers on the *Brazos* took a liking to August. She invited him to attend a dinner and dance at her father's plantation that evening. How could a boy turn down such an offer? He had his uniform cleaned and pressed, the brass buttons shined up. He waited for the carriage to take him to the ball.

It was held at a large plantation house. When August walked in, there were servants everywhere. They offered him bites of food and glasses of refreshment all night long. He had never been waited on by servants before.

It was such a delightful evening. Everyone was so elegantly dressed, the food outstanding, the company agreeable. But now, suddenly, the memory of the black men and women who had served him came rushing back. And for the first time he realized the terrible fact.

They called them "servants." But they weren't servants. They were slaves! No one was going to pay them for their work. And if any of them complained, they wouldn't be fired. They'd be sold off!

He felt ashamed and angry at himself.

The next morning, Captain Chubb was at the wheel, a pipe in his mouth, peering at the stretch of river ahead, when August walked into the pilot house and asked to have a word.

"What's bothering you, greenhorn?" the captain asked.

"I want to be put ashore at the next landing."

"Ashore?" Chubb said. He turned around and faced August. "Whatever for?"

"I need to go back to St. Louis."

"Can't it wait?"

August looked down at his boots.

"I can't explain it to you, Cap'n. I need to sort some things out."

Chubb said nothing for a while.

"Is this about what happened last night?"

"Yes ... I mean, no, sir," he said.

He really didn't want to talk with Chubb about slavery. He knew where he stood on the matter. *He'll just tell me to leave politics to the politicians. And if a politician ever steps on our boat, I'm supposed to check my wallet before he steps off. Ha ha.*

"What I mean is," August continued, "I've been thinking about my life here on the river. I've had a real good time riding the *Brazos.* But I've realized that life is about more than just having a good time. So I need to step off here and chart myself a new course."

Chubb nodded thoughtfully.

"I'll be sorry to lose you, son. But I can't keep you from doing what you need to do."

The two men said nothing more. They shook hands, then August went below and packed his knapsack. At the next landing he walked down the gangplank alone. As the boat moved away he turned and saw Captain Tom Chubb waving from the pilot house.

"Good luck, greenhorn!" he called out.

August watched until the *Brazos* disappeared around a bend in the river. The wake of the steamboat slowly vanished. Only the sound of the whistle lingered in his ears.

KANSAS

When he returned to St. Louis, he discovered his parents were gone and his sister was married. Chaia offered her brother a room in her new house. "Father had a business offer in Kentucky," she explained. "He was planning to send you a letter, but he wasn't sure where to send it. Are you going to stay in St. Louis?"

"I haven't decided," August said.

"You're welcome to stay here as long as you like," Chaia said.

He went to work with his friend Jacob Benjamin. Jacob was seventeen, with a moon face and a round belly. He lived with his parents and helped his father run a dry goods store in the German section. Store work was still boring, but August liked being around Jacob. It was like having a kid brother.

"Did you kill any rattlesnakes when you were in Texas?" Jacob asked him one day.

"Sure, I killed a few."

"With your hands?"

"No, dummy — with my gun. I can hit a scorpion at twenty paces. Or could, anyway."

Jacob's eyes widened. "Really? Could you teach me that?"

"I guess. But we'd have to go somewhere for target practice."

"Are you going back to Texas?"

"No. Not for a while, anyway. I'm going someplace, though. Just haven't decided."

"Will you take me with you?"

August laughed. "Sounds like someone is itching to get out from under the old man's thumb."

Jacob blushed.

"It's just that Father and Mother are happy to have this store and their tidy little home here in the city. I'm happy that they're happy. But then I hear you talk about life out on the prairie and the big open sky and the fresh air. And I think, *that's* where I'd like to be."

"Me too, Jacob. But I haven't found the right opportunity yet."

"When you do, August, will you let me know?"

"Of course."

One of the few things August liked about being back in St. Louis was having access to Northern newspapers again. The slavery issue was heating up in the Congress, and Southern newspapers had their own special way of covering it.

He was scanning the *New York Tribune* one morning at Jacob's store when his eyes landed on a double-decker headline:

KANSAS-NEBRASKA BILL PASSES!

•

WILL SLAVERY EXTEND TO THE PACIFIC?

August read the story with growing alarm.

"Congress has sent to President Pierce for his signature the infamous bill that will open the Indian territory to white settlement. Now the matter of whether Kansas will enter the Union as a free state or a slave state is entrusted to the popular vote."

He set down his newspaper.

"Kansas," he said out loud.

"Come again?"

August looked up. Jacob was across the room, counting inventory.

"I'm going to Kansas."

Jacob stopped counting. He walked over to August.

"Kansas?" Jacob asked. "Why Kansas?"

"Because they've opened it for settlement, and they're going to need a barricade against the men who want to turn it into a slave state. Write this down."

As August dictated his list of provisions, Jacob scribbled them on a scrap of paper.

"I'll need a month's supply of food ... a Colt pistol ... some cartridges and gunpowder ... an ax ... a saw ... and nails. I'm sure I'll think of more things before I leave."

"I'm sure you will," Jacob said, "but already I can think of one thing you're missing."

"What's that?" August asked.

Jacob smiled.

"A business partner!"

August checked himself in a mirror. He had begun growing a beard on the *Brazos.* It filled in his face the length of his cheekbones, making him look years older. He took in the rest of the picture. He had on knee-length boots and a long, heavy jacket. A Colt revolver swung from his belt.

I declare, August Bondi, you've turned yourself into a Missouri roughneck.

His riding partner was a different story. Jacob's short, stubby legs poked out on either side of his horse. Every time August looked back at him, he couldn't help but laugh.

"What?" Jacob said.

"You look like you learned to ride about five minutes

ago," August said, still laughing.

"Ho ho ho. I came to this *country* five minutes ago, remember?"

"Yes, I remember, Jacob."

That was their story as they rode across Missouri. August would tell people that he had just come up from Texas and made friends with Jacob, a German immigrant who was brand new to this country and spoke no English. In reality, the Benjamins had lived in St. Louis since Jacob was six and he spoke English flawlessly. But this way August would do all the talking — which both of them agreed was for the best.

At the first creek bed, Jacob tumbled right off his mount and into the water.

"You all right?" August called out.

"Ja, sehr gut," Jacob sputtered as he stood up.

For days they rode cautiously and went to sleep with painful saddle sores. Then, slowly, they began to pick up speed. One day they made forty-five miles. As the sun was setting they spotted a large farmhouse.

A properly dressed black woman answered the door and fetched the man of the house. He looked like he had stepped off a Louisiana plantation. He wore a crisp shirt, string tie, white coat and straw hat.

"Howdy," August said.

"Evening, gentlemen," he said. "Are you looking for accommodations tonight?"

"Ja!" said Jacob, forgetting that he wasn't supposed to

understand English.

"What my German friend means is, we would be most appreciative of your hospitality. We would be more than happy to compensate you for your trouble."

"Oh, think nothing of it. A little Southern hospitality is what we like to offer to our visitors. Where you headed?"

"Well, we aim to find some choice land in Kansas and stake a claim before everything is taken."

"Mm hmm," said the Missourian. "Now, where did you say you come from, sir?"

"I come from Texas. Round Galveston way, though I spent time in Houston and points in between."

"Mm hmm," the Missourian repeated. He was taking a second look at both of them.

Smile, Jacob, August thought. *Look like a dumb German.*

As the Missourian looked at Jacob, he broke into a huge, goofy grin.

"Say, what's that river that's down by Galveston? They just opened that for riverboat travel not too long ago, didn't they?"

He was testing August.

"You mean the Brazos or the Trinity river?" August said coolly. "I'm familiar with them both."

The Missourian relaxed.

"Oh, I suppose I mean the Brazos. Say, listen, boys, I don't mean to interrogate you or anything, but we've been getting a lot of reports of Yankee Negro thieves coming into Missouri and making off with our slaves.

They take them over to Kansas and then shuttle them off to so-called freedom. It's a great concern to everyone around here. Because it's just outright thievery, that's what it is! Why, most of the Negroes out in this part of Missouri have a good life. They don't work in cotton fields or the sugar mills. Look at Lucy here. She works exclusively with Mrs. Johnson in the household."

Lucy, who was setting the table, did not look up.

August nodded sympathetically. "I've heard those same stories," he said. "We been keepin' an eye out for them, too."

"Ja," said Jacob, nodding his head.

After they had dropped their bags, the weary travelers came down for supper.

"Lucy will serve you boys," the Missourian said. "Mrs. Johnson and I had our meal before you arrived. We'll see you two in the morning."

"Much obliged, sir. Good night."

"Guten nacht."

An upstairs door closed. At that moment the door from the kitchen swung open. Lucy walked briskly into the room holding a pot of coffee. For the first time all night, she spoke.

"I hope it is not too impertinent for me to ask, gentlemen," she said in a low voice, "but is you goin' to Kansas for any other reason than to claim some of that fine, fine prairie for yourselves?"

August was taken aback. He wasn't sure what to say.

Then he realized: *She waited until they went to bed.*

"Um, well, miss," he said quietly, "we thought it would be good to set up a nice welcoming committee for any Missourians who might want to come over and ... *visit* our fair territory."

"I expect that would be a very useful thing to do," she said, watching the coffee as she poured it into their cups. "Mr. Johnson likes to talk about those Yankee slave stealers, but meanwhile he and those border ruffians are tryin' to make Kansas safe for slavers like himself."

She stopped pouring and looked at August with piercing eyes.

"But mark my words, these are soft people. Why, Mr. Johnson, he ain't shot so much as a pheasant in twenty years. If you happen to know any free-state folk, you tell 'em, they just need to *take a stand.* They just take a stand and these border ruffians gonna high tail it right back to Missouri!"

And with that she marched back into the kitchen.

August and Jacob looked at each other, then ate the rest of their meal in stunned silence.

The green prairies of Kansas Territory stretched out for mile after unbroken mile. On that windy afternoon the tallgrass undulated like ocean waves. They stopped and took in the sight.

"Who could make a living farming such a country?" said Jacob.

"I suppose we'll find out," said August.

Before leaving St. Louis, he and Jacob had spoken with a traveler who had just returned from Kansas. The traveler said there was still good land along the Marais des Cygnes River and Mosquito Branch Creek. They went there to find a claim. They found the river easily, then rode to the first cabin to get directions to the creek.

Before August could dismount, a tall lean man approached him toting a rifle.

"Where you from, stranger?" the man asked.

"St. Louis," August answered.

"That don't mean a thing. What are you doing here? What's your business?"

August hadn't thought of this. Now that they were in Kansas, they were just as likely to run into a free-state settler as a Missourian.

Telling him I'm from Texas might do us more harm than good.

"Well?" said the stranger.

August frowned. Finally he said, "Don't you think it's bad manners to ask someone where they're from without doing the same yourself?"

"I'm from here," the man said testily.

"Where were you from before that?"

"Vermont! What's it to you?"

A Vermont Yankee.

August smiled and extended his hand. "Well, good to meet you, Vermont. I'm your new neighbor."

His name was Baker. After apologizing for the rude welcome, he invited the travelers into his little cabin. It was twelve feet square and furnished with a bed, a table, two chairs, and an oversized trunk. Two bare-footed children hugged their mother's leg and stared at the visitors. The woman offered them a drink of water and a seat at the table.

"We've been getting a lot of slavers around here — most of them from Missouri," said Baker. "They cross over, tack a claim on a tree, and vote in our elections. That's what they did. Just clear out *stole* the election. They aim to make this a slave state, but it's not going to happen. Not over my dead body it won't."

The Vermonter stripped off his shirt. His wife turned away. There were big scars across his back.

"They tied me to a tree and whupped me," he said. "Told me to clear out. But as you can see, I'm still here. They'll get a surprise if they show up again." He looked at August's pistol. "Don't you fellows have rifles?"

"Just this Colt."

"Boys, you need something a little more appropriate to the climate." He walked over to a long box on the floor, pulled out a rifle and handed it to August.

"We got a shipment in the other day. I haven't had the time to hand them all out. People in the East sent them here. This here Sharps rifle is a darn sight better than an old musket, I can tell you that."

The men thanked Baker and took their leave. They rode on and found Mosquito Creek. They picked out two claims. Both had access to water and timber. The next day they rode to the land office and registered their claims.

"So far, so good," Jacob said as they left the office.

They cleared August's claim first. That took the better part of two days. Jacob had never done this kind of work before. Soon he was sporting painful blisters on both hands.

"First I ride a horse," Jacob said. "Now I chop wood and clear land, and I ache everywhere!"

"Don't stop now," said August. "It's making you stronger by the day. Besides, you've got a store to build. You'll be standing behind a counter and getting fat again before you know it."

It took two weeks to put up their first cabin. The building wasn't much to look at, but it was better than sleeping in a tent. After putting a cabin on the Benjamin claim, Jacob returned to St. Louis to load up with items for sale. August spent his days working around the claim. He slept with his Sharps rifle close at hand.

PATE

One afternoon toward the end of the week he saw a horseman ride into the clearing. The man dismounted. He was short and stocky, with hard eyes and a black mustache. He wore a broad felt hat with the crown pushed in.

The spurs of his boots jingled as he walked up to August. He stood there, thumbs hooked in his revolver belt, looking the settler up and down.

"Afternoon," August said pleasantly.

The short man looked up at him.

"You don't know me," he said, "but you'll know soon enough. You come from St. Louis, I hear. Aim to settle down in the territory, do you?"

"News travels fast," August said.

"Anyway, I thought I'd just drop by and give you a little friendly advice."

You're not my friend, August thought.

"There's a heap o' trouble in these parts. But I reckon as soon as we get the free staters out of Kansas, things will look up. If you aim to stay, just tend your own business and keep your mouth shut."

"I've already talked to Baker," August said. "You must be one of the pack of cowards that whipped him. I'm surprised you dared to come here without a dozen border ruffians behind you."

The stranger spat in the dust. "I don't like the way you talk, son. I figured one good Missouri boy was worth a dozen o' your kind."

"I *am* from Missouri," August said. "Now get off my claim."

The man swung into his saddle and turned the horse's head quickly. "Looks like you're going to need a lesson like old Baker!" the stranger said, then galloped off.

"Sounds like Pate," Baker said later. "Henry Clay Pate, a would-be wannabe coulda-been. Drifted around Virginia, Kentucky, Ohio, then got it into his head that he was going to ride into Kansas and capture it for the cause of slavery. He's a coward. I'm sure of it. He doesn't fight fair. He'll try to ambush you. Be careful."

August began sleeping in his clothes with both his Sharps and his Colt.

Four nights later he woke suddenly to the sound of

galloping hoof beats. He sat up and listened.

They're coming from the creek bottom.

In a few minutes he would be able to see them. Holding the Sharps in the crook of his arm, August went outside and stood in the clearing for a moment. The moon had become clouded. He thought he saw movement in the trees. All was silent.

He decided the best place to make a stand was just inside the door frame. He could see them without their seeing him.

A horse nickered in the distance. The men had dismounted and were walking their horses closer to avoid detection. August counted six shadows.

Suddenly one of the horsemen mounted and charged. Two more riders spurred their horses toward the side of the cabin. August laid his cheek against the comb of the butt and pulled the trigger.

A horse reared and snorted. The attackers began galloping around the cabin and whooping. Someone lit a torch and tossed it into the clearing. It fell just short of the door. A second torch struck the cabin but the wall did not immediately burst into flames. The wood of the cabin was still wet.

August reloaded his rifle in the dark and fired. Bullets whistled around the doorway. Flames from the torch began to spread. A bullet caught August on the shoulder. He winced and dropped the Sharps rifle. Taking the Colt pistol from his belt, he began firing into the darkness. Above the sound of gunfire and pounding hoof beats he heard Pate command his raiders to close in.

Then the number of hoof beats doubled. Horses seemed to be everywhere.

Did he bring an army? August thought.

But then the shooting stopped and a man burst into the cabin. August was raising his gun when the man called out, "Hold your fire, friend! You wouldn't want to shoot a free-state neighbor, would you?"

He stripped off his jacket and began beating at the flames. "Got an ax?"

August tried to stand up. The stranger saw he was wounded and waved his hand. "Never mind, I'll find it," he said.

More men rushed in and joined the furious slapping effort. Others began chopping away the burning frame-work. "Sorry to hack up your shanty," the first man said, wiping his perspiring forehead. "But it's better than losing all of it."

The men were dressed in work clothes and boots. One had a crippled left arm and held a pistol in his right hand, like August.

A younger man charged into the cabin. "We got 'em on the run, Jason!" he yelled. "They didn't even know what happened!"

"Good," said Jason. "Now let's see to our friend here. Owen, you go heat some water, but do it outside. We had plenty of fire in here. Oliver, get that wound dressed as best you can."

August tried to get up again. "I can look after myself," he said. Then he groaned and slumped to the ground.

"Get him outside, boys," Jason said. August felt strong hands take him by the arms and legs and gently carry him onto the porch. He felt a great weariness come over him. He closed his eyes for a moment.

When he opened them again, he was back inside the cabin. Through the charred shanty door he could see streaks of dawn. His left arm had been neatly bandaged and the pain had become tolerable. His three rescuers sat cross-legged on the dirt floor, watching him.

August raised himself on one elbow and smiled, "Well, gentlemen, you've done me a good turn."

"Just being neighborly," Jason said. "Been meaning to pay you a visit ever since you come to the territory. Last night seemed as good a time as any."

He put his arms around the shoulders of the two younger men. "You're looking at three members of the Brown tribe." He nodded toward his brothers. "This rapscallion's name is Owen. That one's Oliver. And there's more of us, seven in all, though we ain't all in Kansas. The others are on their way, including our old man."

August looked into the faces around him. Jason was gaunt and bearded, with stony gray eyes. Owen was red-haired with a cheerful, open expression, and had a withered arm hanging at his side. Oliver was as tall as Jason, but his features were pale and sensitive. August felt at home with them immediately.

"We heard a little about you from Baker," Jason went on. "Heard you were a bit of a firebrand."

"As you can see," August said, casting a glance over at the burned-out doorway. "Anyway, I'm glad Baker talked me up to you boys. I believe it saved my life."

"Well, he said you're one of us. And I reckon the Old Man will take a liking to you."

"Who is the Old Man?" August asked.

Jason gave a short laugh. "*Who* is he? Or *what* is he? It ain't always easy to tell. Sometimes he's like a rock. Sometimes he's more like an old eagle. He can be like a mother too. I seen him nurse Owen through a fever, gentle as a woman. I seen him with tears in his eyes when one of his lambs got ate by a wolf. And I seen him other ways."

"Where is he now?"

"Up in New York," Jason said. "But he's making his way here, along with Salmon and Watson. And when he gets here things are going to start happening. Pate and his gang got a hard lesson to learn. And the Old Man's a good teacher."

"We don't dare call him 'the Old Man' to his face," Owen said.

"He's our father," Jason said. "John Brown."

THEO

Jacob was back. Not on a horse this time, but driving a wagon loaded with provisions. Beside him sat a giant of a man, with heavy shoulders and massive arms, dressed as if he had just come from a wedding. A black string tie was knotted tightly around his collar. Instead of boots, he wore soft shoes that had been polished until they gleamed. A neatly folded coat lay on his lap. Jacob Benjamin looked like a hardened frontiersman next to this newcomer.

August dropped his ax and ran to greet them. Jacob climbed stiffly from the wagon. The stranger followed, stepping gingerly as if he feared to scuff his shoes.

"This is Theo Wiener," Jacob said, "A new partner for us. I told him, 'Wiener, this is a savage wilderness fit only for hard men like myself and August! Stay in St. Louis.' But he insisted."

August shook hands with Theo. "Glad to have you," he said. "But I disagree with my friend here. Kansas isn't savage wilderness, though it's savage in other ways."

"Yes, I have heard of troubles here," Theo said slowly. "But I trust the newspapers were exaggerating. For them there is always the need to sell papers."

August led the way to the cabin and pointed out the repairs.

"All this was burned in the middle of the night by border ruffians," he said. "And *I'm* not exaggerating. There were six men here. Six against one! If it wasn't for some of our free-state friends who rode to my rescue, I might have been burned out — or worse."

The big man nodded his head gravely. "I suppose there will always be incidents," Theo said.

Incidents?

"Theo, I don't think you understand. There's a *war* brewing out here, not just 'incidents.' In St. Louis you've got a government to protect you. Out here there is no government. Just you, your gun, and your neighbors."

"Oh, come now, Bondi," said Theo. "You have a government out here. The capital is in Lecompton, is it not? And Jacob tells me there is a land office nearby where you registered your claim. So even out here you have government. And have there not already been elections?"

"Yes, and do you know what happened?" August retorted, his voice rising. "The Missourians, those border ruffians" — he jabbed his finger in the direction of Missouri — "they came over here by the wagonload and cast most of the ballots in our elections. Voted all their people into the legislature. And do you know what kind of laws they're passing now?"

"I suppose you will tell me."

"Yes, I will. Wiener, do you think slavery is a good thing?"

"No, of course not."

"There!" August said, pouncing on his words. "You've just broken the laws of the territory of Kansas."

Theo looked confused.

"The legislature has passed a law prescribing jail time and whippings for anyone who says a bad word about slavery," August said. "Care to guess what the penalty is for helping a slave escape from his so-called master?"

"Jail time?" Theo guessed.

"The sentence for helping a fugitive slave is *death.* Or if they're feeling generous toward you, ten years of hard labor. That's what passes for democracy here in Kansas. Want to know the best part, Theo?"

Theo started to shift about awkwardly on his feet.

"The president of the United States sent his own man here to make sure those bogus laws, passed by our bogus legislature, are enforced. We've got a president that is as much a pro-slavery man as any border ruffian."

Theo looked shocked. "You shouldn't say things like

that about the president," he said.

"It's true!" retorted August, his eyes flashing. "The South has President Pierce under its thumb! His secretary of war is Jeff Davis — a Mississippi slave owner!"

The anger went out of August's voice. He put a hand on the big man's shoulder.

"Where did you come from, Theo? Where did you live before you came to America?"

"Poland. "

"In the *shtetl*?"

"Yes."

"You mentioned the 'incidents' here in Kansas," August said. "Were there 'incidents' in the *shtetl*? In Poland?"

Theo suddenly looked hurt.

"Yes, there were incidents."

"Were there reprisals against you and your family? Your people?"

Theo looked sadly at August.

"Why do you think we came to America?" he said. "They killed my uncle Josef and ..."

He looked off in the distance.

"... my nephew, Lionel, too. We were the same age."

Theo composed himself, then looked back fiercely at August.

"But that was *different.* In Poland we were an oppressed people. In America we are free! Here there are no *shtetls*. I can live where I want. I can do what I want, I can wear decent clothes, I can go where I choose. The politics don't concern me. Let them do what they please. I have no quarrel here."

August leaned in close, so close he could hear Theo breathing heavily.

"The quarrel is here already, Theo," he said slowly. "Yes, you are an American now. And you have the right to make your own decisions as an American."

Theo looked at August. He seemed to be thinking it over.

"I choose to take no sides," he finally said.

You're walking in a dream, August thought.

The three men began construction of a store building. The Brown brothers rode over most days to lend a hand. In a short while the work was done. It stood on Jacob's claim, some distance from the cabin. On a long piece of board, Jacob cut a sign and filled in the letters with charcoal: BENJAMIN & CO.

He looked at the sign proudly. "You should excuse me, August, that I didn't put your name there too, but I thought I was going to run out of board."

August laughed. "You'll be in the store more than I will. Call it anything you want."

Theo stood with his hands on his hips, watching Benjamin install the sign above the entrance. When the little man clambered down, Theo stepped back and surveyed the store approvingly. "Almost finished," he said.

Jacob turned to Theo. "Almost? It *is* finished!" he said.

"I carried this all the way from St. Louis." He drew a

small metal tube from his pocket. "How can you say the store is finished without this?"

It was a *mezuzah.* Inside the tube was a tiny replica of a passage from the Torah: *And these words which I command thee this day shall be in thine heart ... and thou shalt write them upon the posts of thy house.* August watched while the two men nailed the little container to the door post.

Suddenly, his mind raced back to Vienna. To the family's last few hours there. Perhaps the saddest moment on that sad day was when Father got up on a chair and took down the *mezuzah*. Now the symbol of his faith was here. And somehow, the memories of those last months came back and did not sting like they once did.

Heinrech is here with me now, he thought. *And so is Anschl.*

"All right," Theo announced, "*now* we are ready for business!"

They moved the provisions into the store and set up a rough wooden counter to serve customers. Besides barrels of flour, grain, preserves, crackers, and salt, Jacob had acquired bolts of cloth, a few tools, and some jars of licorice and hard candies. When they were done, he could hardly contain his excitement.

"It looks like a store," Jacob said. "It *smells* like a store. There's nothing like it from here to St. Louis!"

While Jacob occupied himself with keeping the books and inventory, Theo did most of the actual storetending. August pitched in on busy days. The big man was always polite, always soft spoken and ready to oblige. But whenever two men in the store started talking politics, Theo moved away and said nothing. August thought he looked uncomfortable.

"I don't get your new man," Baker said one day. "He ain't free-state, and he ain't slave state. So what is he?"

"He's a man making up his mind," August reassured him. "Give him time. With his size and strength, he'll be a great asset to us one day."

Since Pate's raid on August's cabin, the area around Marais des Cygnes had been calm. August heard rumors of pro-slavery gangs gathering on the Missouri side. Mostly, though, it seemed to him the area was filling up with free-state settlers. Like Theo, they didn't take the newspaper reports too seriously before arriving in Kansas. But within a week or two, the man of the house would ride up to Baker's house or the Brown claim and inquire about replacing his squirrel gun with a more accurate and powerful Sharps rifle.

One night, when August was over at the Browns helping clean and assemble a new shipment of guns, another brother rode up. John Brown, Junior, was the biggest and strongest one he had seen yet. His whole face was covered in whiskers, he had keen eyes, and his voice was deep with intensity.

"The Old Man is delayed in New York," he told his brothers. "But he's coming soon."

Business at the store was brisk. Jacob soon had to hire a driver to bring more provisions back from St. Louis.

Even the pro-slavery settlers started coming by Benjamin & Co. One day August was surprised to see Dutch Bill Sherman come through the door. Dutch Bill was a tall, hard-faced farmer from across the creek. August had gotten to know him, since he was the area's mail courier. He had a big mouth and was friend to every Missouri border ruffian who came riding through the area. But August kind of liked Dutch Bill. He knew he could trust his neighbor to safely deliver his letters to St. Louis without tearing them open to read their contents. Still, he was a handful.

Dutch Bill strutted around the store, thumbs hooked in his heavy belt, a dirty straw hat jammed on the back of his head. August thought he smelled like liquor.

Dutch Bill went up to the counter.

"Say boy," he said to Theo. "Where's the corn meal?"

"Um ... we will have more corn meal in the shipment that arrives on Friday," Theo said. August noticed that his hands were shaking.

Theo, you're twice his size. Don't be intimidated by him.

"Well, isn't that *perfect*," Dutch Bill said disgustedly. "I was told that this store had everything. Now I gotta make another trip here on *Fri-tay* just to get me some corn *mill,*" he said, mocking Theo's accent. "Sure hope it ain't here too late on *Fri-tay,* after you boys are gone off to your Jewish services."

Uh oh, thought August. *That's crossing the line.* But he said nothing. He wanted to see how Theo handled this.

Theo was staring down at the counter. "You didn't have to say that," he mumbled.

"Don't you answer me back, Jewboy," the farmer snapped. "You keep your place, or I'll teach you a lesson you won't forget!"

August noticed a strange expression crossing the big man's face.

Theo looked up calmly at Dutch Bill. "When you insult me as a person," he said slowly, "it makes no difference. I pay no attention. But when you insult me as a Jew —"

The farmer put his hands on the counter and leaned in, getting his face close to Theo's. "And what do you aim to do about it ... *Jew?*"

"I'm going to throw you out," Theo said, so softly that August barely heard it.

Moving faster than August had ever seen him move, Theo walked quickly around the counter and took Dutch Bill by the throat.

"Ulp," Dutch Bill said.

In one easy motion Theo grabbed the farmer's belt with his free hand, and hoisted him off the floor like a sack of potatoes. His other hand took hold of Dutch Bill's shirt collar.

Dutch Bill flailed helplessly. His fists pounded at Theo's muscular frame. But he could not escape the big man's grip. Theo stepped into the doorway and flung Dutch Bill out the door and into the mud a few feet away. He staggered to his feet and made a move toward Theo. Theo's eyebrows flared and he stepped menacingly toward Dutch Bill. The farmer cursed, got on his horse, and left.

After hours, August and Theo sat on the front porch while Jacob closed up shop.

"I had promised myself that I would never lose my temper in the store," Theo said. "But I could stand no more. It has made me realize something important. I have been afraid of these people. And I was willing to obey a law not because I believed it but because I was afraid of it. In the *shtetl* we feared the law. But there is no *shtetl* here. A man makes his own life.

"In the *shtetl* we kept our mouths shut and suffered without a word. I left Poland years ago. Now I have finally left the *shtetl* that was in my own heart."

August put his hand on Theo's arm and said, "We've been waiting for you, brother."

THE OLD MAN

It was night when August heard a horse gallop into the clearing. He took his rifle and went outside. Jason Brown called to him:

"The Old Man's here! He's over at the farm now. Come quickly, he wants to see you."

August saddled his horse and rode after Jason. A strange sensation coursed through his body all the way over to the Brown claim.

In a few minutes they reached the cabin. It looked like it was dark inside. On closer examination, August could see a thin line of light streaming from the window.

"Here, this way," Jason said, and the two men walked through the darkness.

Inside the cabin a candle burned on a rough wooden

table. August noticed pieces of a shop sack covering the window. The small room was filled with people. He recognized Owen and Oliver, but there were others he did not know.

"This is my brother Fred," said Jason. August felt his hand clasped in a powerful grip and looked into the face of another fair-haired giant. There was no mistaking the Browns. "And Watson ... and Salmon ..."

Young John, sitting astride a bench, nodded to August. At the far end of the room August saw the Old Man.

He was tall, as August had expected. He was lean, his face was haggard, his cheekbones sharp and tight against his weathered skin. August could not guess his age. The Old Man might have been fifty or a hundred and fifty. His hair, which must have been blond in his youth, hung toward his shoulders. His beard was long and white, windblown and matted. His hands had veins like knotted ropes. There was a slight stoop to his shoulders.

But the sharp blue eyes made him different from anyone August had ever met. The blue eyes turned to him. They seemed to penetrate his very being, until August felt that the Old Man had seen to the bottom of his heart. John Brown's voice was strong and vigorous. It held August as firmly as if he had gripped him in his knotted hands.

"My sons have spoken about you, Bondi," the Old Man said. "They tell me you are a brave man. Is that so?"

Had anyone else asked that question, August would

have found a ready answer. But the Old Man seemed to be asking a question that went beyond physical bravery. He was asking about something much deeper. August lowered his eyes.

"I intend to fight for what I believe," he said.

"You'll have the opportunity," John Brown said. "I need brave men with me. A few brave men are worth an army, with God's help." His voice turned soft. "Do you know the Holy Scriptures?"

August nodded.

" 'Because I delivered the poor that cried, and the fatherless, and him that had none to help him,' " the Old Man recited from memory. "And Kansas is only the beginning, Bondi."

Looking at the bearded face before him, August saw the blue eyes widen and flash.

"If there is war here," the Old Man said, his voice rising with every word, "there will be *greater* wars in other places. I do not fear it!"

And with that, John Brown fell silent. He sat motionless on the bench, one hand resting on his knee, the other on the shoulder of his eldest son. As if he had fallen into a waking dream, his eyes looked past the flame of the candle toward some great distance visible only to himself.

August stayed a few minutes longer and talked with the others before taking his leave.

As he rode back toward Mosquito Creek, an image of John Brown was fixed in his mind. August imagined him sitting like a patriarch from the Scriptures in the center of a painting, surrounded by his sons.

He had trouble sleeping that night. All he could think about was the Old Man and what he had said.

I delivered the poor ... This is just the beginning ... There will be wars.

It was a prediction of violence, of retribution. Yet August found himself excited by the possibility.

Perhaps John Brown is the man that we've been waiting for. Maybe things are going to start happening now.

August heard the news from one of his neighbors, a schoolteacher from Ohio named John Grant. "Elections!" said Grant. "Those rascals have run out of things to steal. So they've called another election. Now they can steal that, too!"

The free-state men gathered in the Benjamin store to discuss their next move. The Brown brothers were there, as was the Old Man. He sat apart from the others.

Baker spoke first.

"I've seen this happen before," he said. "They want us to vote to make things look legal. But mark my words, on election day them ruffians aim to cross the border again and outvote us."

Grant rose to his feet. "The best thing for us is not to vote at all. I have word from the folks in Lawrence that we're going to have our own elections. And more than that, we're going to have our own constitution. When we vote, we'll vote in a free election. Until then, stay away from the polls!"

Afterward, Theo asked August, "Does that mean we'll have two governments for the territory?"

"That's what it sounds like," said August.

"Sounds confusing."

"I'd rather have two governments than the one we have now."

The second election was, as predicted, won by Missourians who streamed into Kansas to cast their ballots. Not long after, the Old Man showed up at August's claim.

"If we're going to raise up a free-state government, we will need an army to back it up," Brown said. "We need men who hate slavery. Men who will stand firm against the ruffians."

"I agree," said August.

"If you can find men like that and sign them up, I'll make sure they have rifles."

"You'll have your men," August said.

In the days that followed, he and Theo and Jason Brown rode far over the territory. Finding free-state claims was easy. Finding recruits for John Brown's militia was not. Many of the settlers told August they thought the trouble would soon blow over.

The winter of 1856 was a hard one, and all was quiet on the prairie. But then, around the beginning of May, free-state scouts reported to August that Missourians had been sighted once more gathering on the border with Kansas. August began staying up nights, tense and alert, Sharps rifle at his side. It reminded him of his first days in the territory. Often he would wake, imagining the Old Man had called him. But there was no sound of men or guns, only the owls in the woods.

13 POTTAWATOMIE

Baker came charging into the Bondi claim on his horse. "They've burned down Lawrence!" he yelled.

August could only get the barest details from him — the Eldridge Hotel up in smoke, the presses of the free-state newspaper thrown in the river, buildings looted, windows broken.

"We rally at Brown's farm. Bring any rations you have!" Baker kicked his heels against the horse's flanks and sped down the road toward the next claim.

The call to action had come at last, as August knew it would. He moved quickly, helping Theo and Jacob load the wagon with goods from the store. Jacob hitched up the wagon as August and Theo checked rifles and cartridges. Dusk was falling rapidly. First to the Brown farm, then on to Lawrence. It would be an all-night march. "Ride the wagon, Jacob," August said. "Theo and I will take the gray pony. We'll change off later. We've got a long ride ahead of us."

August pressed on as quickly as he dared without exhausting the horses. At the Brown farm, they found Junior forming three dozen militiamen into columns. Even in the failing light August could distinguish him easily, a powerful figure, taller than the rest.

"The Old Man's gone to Middle Creek," Junior said. "Jay and Owen are with him. We'll rally there and push on to Lawrence." His face was flushed with excitement. "For once we can stand up to the Missourians like men!"

By ten o'clock August and the company of militia reached Middle Creek. The Old Man was there, and August noticed the difference immediately. To August he had transformed into a leader of men. The signs of age had left him, his body was strong and taut. He stood erect, shouting orders to those around him. "Move out, boys! We can't keep the Missouri gentlemen waiting."

A little after dawn the militia reached the outskirts of Lawrence. Ahead August could see black smoke rising from the charred town. He dismounted and Theo joined him. For a moment the two men just stood silently, watching the dark clouds.

The Old Man deployed the militia and prepared to enter the town. Before they had gone another hundred yards August saw a horseman galloping across the fields. It was John Grant.

"You can't reach town," Grant said breathlessly. "There's government troops in there."

"Troops?" Theo said. He seemed puzzled. "Did they hold off the ruffians?"

"They didn't hold off anybody," Grant said. "They came in after the town was half burnt to the ground. Then the colonel gave orders that both sides have to break up. The ruffians went back across the border. Most of 'em, anyway. The U.S. Army's got men all around the town, so unless you can fight your way through, there's no way to help Lawrence."

The Old Man was silent, looking toward the town, smoke and fires burning everywhere.

"That's not all," said Grant. "We got trouble enough back at our own claims. The slavers were out last night, burning and raiding every claim where there wasn't a man at home to defend it. Any man they knew was out with the militia, I don't imagine they left his cabin standing, unless his wife was there to plead her case."

The Old Man turned to face the others. August saw that his whole body was trembling.

"We strike back this time!" Brown yelled. "A blow they will never forget! They'll learn once and for all they can't drive us out!"

He fell silent.

His eyes scanned the faces of the men assembled before him.

"I want half a dozen of you," Brown said. "No more."

Without hesitation, August and Theo stepped forward, as did Fred and Salmon Brown and some farmers from the militia. The Old Man put his hand on August's shoulder.

"You follow later. I need you to bring us rations and whatever news you can find out after this is over."

"After what is over?" August asked.

"The work I must do," said Brown. "Meet me tomorrow night at Middle Creek. There's an empty cabin near the big patch of brush along the bank. We'll be there."

There was a look on Brown's face that August had never seen before — a look of blind, cold fury. The rest of the militiamen loaded into a wagon. As it creaked down the trail, August looked back at the Old Man. Even from a hundred away he could see the figure shaking with rage.

"I have a pretty good idea of what he has in mind," August said to Jacob.

"What is that?"

"That Scripture he likes to quote. 'Vengeance is mine, saith the Lord.' "

The militia camped near Lawrence for the night. The next day, while Jacob stayed with the others, August hitched up the wagon and started back for his rendezvous with John Brown.

When he reached Middle Creek, he turned the wagon off the trail. Suddenly a figure loomed out of the darkness and seized the bridle. Another shape rose from the brush.

"Halt!" a strange voice called out.

Then a more familiar one said, "Hold your fire, I know him." It was Theo. August climbed down from the wagon quickly.

"How is the Old Man?"

"He's in the cabin," Theo said. "All day he has been sitting alone. Last night he was like a madman. Now he has hardly spoken to us."

Theo looked down.

"It was a terrible thing he did," he said. "Believe me, August, I am not thinking of the right or wrong. When I came to the territory I had no desire to fight. I changed my mind. I will fight for the Old Man, no matter what he has done. But I am still glad I had no part in it."

"No part in what?" August said. "Theo, tell me, what has he done?"

Theo shook his head. "When we left you we headed for Pottawatomie. The Old Man was raging. He kept telling us that we were going to protect our homes. But we weren't heading to our homes.

"At Pottawatomie he told me to ride behind as a guard. He passed out sabers to the rest. Then we went from one claim to the next—wherever a slaver had a cabin. Maybe half a dozen altogether. It was over very quickly. Old Brown caught them as soon as they came outside. He never laid a hand on the women or children. But the men had no mercy from him."

"What men? You mean, Dutch Bill and Pate?"

"No," Theo said. His voice was very quiet now. "Doyle ... Wilkinson ... two others, just boys really, couldn't have been more than eighteen."

Theo looked up. But he was looking past August, as if in a trance. "He killed them all in cold blood. *An eye for an eye,* the Old Man said. *A tooth for a tooth.* But these weren't Missourians. They were Kansans, like us. They didn't own slaves. They didn't have anything to do with Lawrence."

"No," said August. "But they lived out by the creek, where no one would hear their screams for help."

Theo's trance broke. He turned and looked at August.

"Where will it end?" he asked. "The lives of half a dozen men? The ruffians have killed more. That isn't the point. But to take vengeance like that?" The big man's voice faltered.

August left Theo and went toward the small cabin. He pushed open the door. The Old Man was seated on the floor in a corner of the room, his arms clasped about his knees, his gray head resting against the wall. A Bible lay open on the table beside a gutted candle.

"I've brought you food," August said. "All that is left."

The Old Man raised his head. "Share it out as far as it goes." He looked sharply at August. "You've heard about Pottawatomie by now. I can tell by your face. Do you doubt that justice was done?"

August did not answer for a moment. The Old Man

went on. "I have examined my conscience," he said. "With the help of the Lord, I have done what had to be done. I fight as an instrument of the Lord's vengeance. Slavery is a sin. And there is no remission of sin without the shedding of blood!" The Old Man's voice rose higher and his eyes blazed.

"But Doyle was an innocent man," August said. "He never fought against us."

"He believed in slavery," Brown cried. "He believed in the great evil of this country. Every free-state man in Kansas will say I have carried out justice. Are you to be the only one against me?"

"Just because I would not have done the same thing," said August, "does not mean I am against you. We are fighting on the same side. If I do not agree with you, I do not judge you."

"Then you will stay with me?"

Once again August saw the power in the Old Man's eyes. The power of a whirlwind.

"I'll stay with you," he answered.

The two men stepped out of the cabin. In the dawn August saw the lined and weary faces of Theo, Fred Brown, and the others.

"All right, boys," said the Old Man, who sounded tired. "I'm sending Bondi back to find out what news he can. The rest of us stay until we hear from him."

August turned the horses around and drove in the direction of Marais des Cygnes. A quarter mile from the claim he saw Baker riding toward him. The Vermonter's face was bruised, blackened with powder, his shirt torn. "Where's the Old Man?" Baker called breathlessly.

"Near Middle Creek," August said. "What happened to you? Did the militia get back?"

Baker reined in his mount. "Some of us are back. The Old Man's raised a hornet's nest. Pate's got near a hundred men with him now. He's at Black Jack, on his way to Prairie City. And here's the worst — they got two of the Browns!"

BLACK JACK

August felt the blood leave his face. "Which two?"

"Jason and Junior," Baker said. "They didn't take part in the raid from what I hear, but it don't matter. They was Browns, and no questions was asked."

"Are they alive?" August asked.

"More like half alive. Beat near to death. I saw Pate drag 'em away in chains. Half of Pate's gang cut us off on the way back from Lawrence."

"You were cut off?" August exclaimed. "How many got through? What about Jacob Benjamin?"

Baker turned away. "He was with John and Jason. Pate's got him, too. Seems like the whole country's out to find John Brown and anyone else who had a part in those Pottawatomie killings."

As Baker rode off, August turned the wagon and followed. When he reached camp, the Old Man was already on horseback and shouting orders to the rest of the men.

"Leave the wagon!" he yelled to August. "We've got to travel fast."

Theo, riding the gray pony, found a fresh mount for August. They hid the wagon in the brush and tied up August's tired horses near the camp site. The two men rode side by side behind Brown, straining every muscle to keep up with him as he took short cuts through fields and splashed his way across creek beds.

Where does he get the strength? August wondered.

"There's no more than ten of us, and Pate's got at least a hundred," said Theo. "How are we doing this?"

"Follow the Old Man," August said. "He doesn't care how many men Pate has."

And neither do I. We're getting Jacob back.

At Prairie City a crowd of settlers greeted Brown with cheers. A man carrying a saber and pistol came forward.

"Glad you're here, Captain Brown. My name's Shore—captain of the Prairie City Rifles. I have nineteen men. Will you accept command?"

The Old Man nodded. August saw that he was not looking at Shore, but beyond the settlement, past the fields. He spoke in a flat, emotionless voice, his eyes peering at the countryside beyond.

"Tell your men to prepare to attack," Brown said.

"Attack?" Captain Shore exclaimed. "We can't put more

than thirty men in the field. We barely have enough ammunition for one engagement! My plan was to take up a defensive position around the settlement —"

The Old Man turned on him angrily. "Did you not ask me to take command here?"

Captain Shore stammered. "Yes, captain. But there's so few of us. We can't fight three against one. I can't ask my men to face odds like that."

"But you ask me to do it!" Brown cried. "I have nine men with me and I'll attack with those men. You can follow or not, as you please. We've all wasted enough time sitting like frightened rabbits. This time we strike first."

He marched back to his horse. The others followed. Brown ordered Captain Shore and his rifle company to stay in the rear. The Brown company would advance and make the charge, with Shore coming in to support them when the Old Man gave a signal.

Wordlessly the column galloped from the settlement toward Black Jack. The Old Man called a halt near a stand of trees. They dismounted and picketed the horses. August could make out Shore's rifle company through the trees and brush.

"We go on foot from here," Brown said quietly.

August and Theo followed as the Old Man made his way cautiously through the tall grass, heading for an observation point at the top of the hill. They had only made it a few paces when a volley of shots rang out. Bullets whistled through the dry grass. Now August saw Pate's men clearly. They were gathered in the valley below. Flat against the ground, he slid forward, holding the flintlock in front of him.

John Brown motioned him back. "Stay where you are," he ordered. "I'm going to take a look." He edged forward. The volley began again. Bullets tore into the ground beside August and whistled through the air. He glanced behind at Theo. The big man was having a difficult time keeping his bulk flat against the ground and puffed heavily as he moved forward. But he grinned broadly at August.

"What do you think of Kansas now!" August yelled back at him.

Theo yelled back in Hebrew, *"Sof odom muves!"* ("We all have to go one way or another!")

The Old Man stood. "There's a sunken road at the bottom of the hill. We can use it for a trench. Now, boys! Follow me!" He began to run.

The rifle fire was deafening. Heart pounding, August raced ahead, half stumbling, half running. Everyone reached the sunken road, but two men had taken fire. A young Prairie City volunteer named Carpenter was down on the ground, writhing in pain. At least he was moving. John Brown's son-in-law, Henry Thompson, lay still. But the Old Man was too focused on the battle to care.

"Keep up your fire!" he shouted.

August rested the flintlock against the rim of the trench. The slavers were less than a hundred yards away.

Where is Shore? August wondered. He knew the Old Man was thinking the same thing.

"We can't wait for support!" Brown said. "If we don't get to them first, they'll wipe us out."

At that moment a single horseman charged down the hill at full gallop, straight through the white billows of smoke. Fred Brown! Shouting like a madman, he jumped over the ditch and headed directly for Pate's camp.

Theo cried, "Is he trying to kill himself?"

Waving his hat, Fred Brown galloped in a circle around Pate's men. August heard him yelling, "Come on, boys, we've got them surrounded! This way! Don't let them escape!" The blond giant was calling out orders to an army of imaginary attackers. *Brilliant!*

In moments, August could see men moving around in Pate's camp. Fred rode back in triumph, having gotten the enemy in an uproar.

The Old Man ordered rapid fire.

"They're breaking!" he shouted. "Keep after them!"

He leaped out of the trench and stood upright, his eyes blazing. "Charge the camp!"

August and Theo raced into the midst of Pate's scattering militia. August heard the excited shouts of Oliver. He saw Owen strike a slaver with his one good arm.

Suddenly, a dozen men rushed onto the scene.

"Shore!" August yelled. *About time,* he thought.

Pate's men put up little resistance after that. They began dropping their guns and running.

August caught sight of a figure sneaking through the dead grass, away from the swarm of militia. He sprang forward and seized the figure by the shoulders. The man struggled and rolled away into the dust.

"I surrender! I surrender!"

It was Pate.

Brown strode up and gripped the cowering captain by the shirt front. "Where are my sons? Pate, you murdering coward, if you've harmed a single one of them..."

"They aren't here!" Pate gasped. "I swear they're all right. The government troops made us give them up."

"Don't lie to me!" Brown cried.

"It's true! We had 'em for a while. Second Dragoons took 'em to camp, till they stand trial for what they did at Pottawatomie."

"Not one of those boys had anything to do with that," Brown said. "You're a hostage for their lives, Pate."

Captain Shore appeared, looking sheepish over his late arrival. "My congratulations, captain. It was a brilliant action. And my humble apologies."

"It isn't over yet," Brown said. "My sons are still prisoners." He turned to August. "Ride to Paola as fast as you can and tell the soldiers, if they won't set my boys free, we'll come and take them ourselves."

August galloped up to the U.S. Dragoons' headquarters. A sergeant admitted them to a tent where a group of chained figures sat in the shadows.

It was Jacob who saw August first. With a cry of joy and

relief he stumbled to his feet and embraced August.

"They're going to let me out soon," Jacob said. "They kept us because they thought we were at Pottawatomie. But what about the store? For days all I kept thinking was that I couldn't sweep the floor. The dust will be an inch thick by the time I get back!"

August did not tell Jacob the store had been ruined.

He looked around the tent for young John. Jason pointed to a figure lying in the corner. "The slavers beat him up badly," Jason said. "He'll recover from that. But his mind is gone. He doesn't even know where he is. We'll have to take him out of the territory and let him rest."

August gazed at the battered face of Brown's eldest son. He looked like a broken man, this giant, this leader of the Brown brothers, destroyed beyond recognition.

Jason took August aside and spoke softly to him, so that the sergeant standing guard could not hear.

"Get Theo and the others out of the territory as fast as you can," he said. "Try to get my father out too. There's a reward for anyone who catches them. Five hundred dollars for the Old Man, and a hundred for anybody else at Pottawatomie — dead or alive."

August reported back to the Old Man. Brown's eyes flashed.

"Five hundred dollars is a fair price," he said. "They can try to collect it later. You take care of the prisoner exchange. I'm going north for a few weeks. We need more provisions and money. This campaign isn't over."

"We'll be ready when you come back," August said. They shook hands and the Old Man gave orders to break camp. Theo was silent, his face grave.

"I don't want to leave," he said at last. "I came here afraid to fight. I go without having fought enough."

August put his hand on his friend's shoulder. "It's for the best, Theo. With a price on your head I can't let you take any more risks. Tell everyone in St. Louis I am well, but that we have a long way to go before this is over."

Theo nodded. There were tears in the big man's eyes as he turned his horse and rode away.

August returned to Marais des Cygnes. The Old Man and his sons were gone now, the Brown cabin stood empty. August headed for his own claim.

As he turned into the clearing he was surprised to find that most of the wreckage had disappeared. Then as he reined up he suddenly saw Jacob busy nailing planks to the ruined front of the store.

There was a brand-new BENJAMIN & CO. sign hanging over the door frame.

"A few little alterations and improvements and we'll be back in business," he said cheerfully.

15

OSAWATOMIE

By the end of the month the Old Man was back in the territory. He rode up on a team of horses pulling a wagon loaded down with provisions and weapons.

How does he get all this past the Missourians? August wondered.

That night John Brown spoke to the militiamen.

"There are a thousand ruffians massing on the border," he said. "If we attack at once, we'll throw them off balance and smash them to bits. I beat Pate with ten men! And now, with God's help we'll break the back of the entire ruffian army. The important thing is speed. *Speed!*"

August packed his gear. He had told the Old Man he would be ready and had given his promise to follow him.

"You must stay behind this time, Jacob," August said. "I'll send a couple of militiamen to help you guard the claim."

Jacob looked regretfully at the new cabins and shook his head. "No, I do not stay behind. I'll be sorry if they burn the store again. But we need every man. We started from nothing. We can do it again if we have to."

Brown's company of thirty-five was joined by Captain Cline's forty militiamen. The columns moved forward. The Old Man, in his stained white jacket, with two heavy pistols at his belt, rode at the head. His scouts had told him Osawatomie was most likely the ruffians' target. Brown ordered his columns in that direction. By two in the morning the free-state militia had reached the outskirts of Osawatomie. The Old Man called a halt.

In the heavy darkness August stood guard. Beside him Jacob lay asleep. August had promised to wake up Jacob for his turn at guard, but he didn't feel tired. He waited through the dawn.

Suddenly he heard a rifle shot. Then a volley. Jacob started up, rubbing his eyes. The firing rose in volume, shattering the quiet morning. Under the crackle of the rifles August heard a deep-throated rumble and then a *boom* that stopped his heart. *Cannon!* The pro-slavery men had cannon.

Jacob and August raced for the camp. The noise of battle was full-pitched now. They were close enough to hear the shouts of men, to make out figures racing through the edge of timberland. They passed a still form lying at the side of the road. August stopped for a moment in horror. He recognized the familiar crop of yellow hair and tall, powerful body. August knelt and saw the lifeless face of Fred Brown.

Numb with shock, head throbbing, August ran forward. Behind him Jacob gasped and struggled to keep on. In another few moments they were within the town. Cline's militiamen were scattering through the brush.

Before August could stop one to ask what had happened, the cannon roared again. A tree not that far away from them exploded, sending a thousand splinters in every direction. Across the fields August could see the massed companies of Missourians. Three hundred ... four hundred men or more! The wind whipped at the scarlet banners bearing the insignia of a grinning skull and crossbones. He spotted the squad of gunners loading the cannon.

August seized a militiaman by the arm. "Where's Brown?" he shouted.

The rifleman, his face blackened, shirt soaked with sweat, gestured toward the river.

"What's he doing over there?" said August.

"Ruffians got over there somehow."

The pro-slavery forces were attacking — *from the west!* They were trying to drive the militia back to the river and cut them off there.

August scrambled down the banks. He saw the Old Man now, a pistol in each hand. He had established a firing line along the river in a desperate attempt to cover the militia's retreat. August was at his side in a moment. The Old Man glanced quickly at him. His eyes were blazing, but his voice was cold as ice.

"Make every shot count, boys," the Old Man ordered. He stopped by a kneeling militiaman. "Aim a little bit lower," he told the man calmly. "Aim for the gut, not the head."

The pro-slavery forces had loaded the cannon with grape shot. With each blast, dozens of deadly pellets ripped through the bushes and sang around August's head.

"Hold fast a little longer!" Brown cried.

Gradually the militiamen fell back to the river. In a few more minutes the free-state men would be across and the retreat secured.

"Cross over now!" Brown shouted.

"Go yourself. I'll cover you!" August shouted back.

"Do as you're ordered!" the Old Man screamed.

The militiamen pressed around him and August felt himself pushed into the river. He sought Jacob in vain and struggled to turn back. He saw John Brown wade into the water, his white jacket floating behind, his two pistols held aloft. Now only a few men were left on the bank, continuing to fire. Then they too put up their rifles and plunged into the river. The last man to cross was Jacob Benjamin. Bullets churned the water around him. For a moment Jacob stumbled, then regained his balance. August hauled his soaked and breathless friend up the bank.

"I held them off as long as I could," Jacob yelled over the chaos. "I would have stayed, but I ran out of ammunition!"

"It's a good thing you did," August told him, "or you'd have been a dead hero instead of a live one!"

With the safety of the river between them and the enemy, the militiamen slowly drew back from the bank. As they reached higher ground the Old Man stopped and looked toward the town. A sheet of flames rose high in the air, pale red in the morning sunlight. Osawatomie was burning.

The Old Man stood weeping, tears streaking the furrows in his lined face. He stretched his open hands toward the blazing town. His parched lips moved but no sound came. August took his arm and led him away.

"There's nothing more you can do," he said gently.

John Brown sat apart from the rest after the battle, alone and silent with his grief.

August returned to the claim with Jacob. The store had been untouched. For the first time in months August rested.

Two weeks after the battle of Osawatomie, Baker found August working in a field. Baker was grinning.

"Truce!" he said. "The ruffians called a truce."

August looked puzzled. "How so?"

"There's too many of us. Too many free-state men willing to defend Kansas. Those border raids ain't working like they used to. Ruffians took heavy casualties at Osawatomie. They were expecting to march straight through to Topeka and take John Brown home as their prisoner."

August smiled. "I see he's mighty popular with the Eastern newspapers. You'd think from reading the *New York Tribune* that we won Osawatomie."

"Maybe we did!" Baker said, as he rode off.

One morning toward the end of September, August noticed a solitary rider making his way slowly up the trail. It was John Brown. August had not seen him since the battle. His face was pale and drawn, his cheeks sunken. His eyes were still keen, but they held a frightening new expression, as if the Old Man were in pursuit of some strange dream.

He reined up his horse. August went to greet him. Brown wasted no time with small talk.

"I'm leaving the territory," he said. "My work here is done."

August looked at him in surprise. The Old Man continued. "I told you once," he said, "that this was only a beginning. That there will be greater wars. Kansas will be free. It is only a matter of time now. But there are other places. Other people. In this country there are millions of souls in bondage. I shall free them. Make a mighty army of them." The voice of the Old Man grew louder. "All over the South the slaves shall rise up!"

He can't be serious, August thought.

"Will you come with me?" Brown asked.

He IS serious.

August waited a moment, collecting his thoughts.

"I have followed wherever you have led," he began. "Now you say your work here is done. But I believe our work here is just beginning. Someday there will be peace. We must build toward that peace. So far there has been only destruction. Building is more important to me. We have a lot of work to do."

"There will be no peace," said the Old Man. "Only a sword." He looked straight at August with his piercing eyes.

"The territory has no valid constitution," August said. "We fought those who would make Kansas a slave state. Now we must fight for our own government. How can I leave now? My work is here."

The Old Man regarded him coldly.

"Good-bye, then," he said. They shook hands.

John Brown turned his horse around and rode away on the trail. August watched until he was out of sight.

FREE STATE

Jacob Benjamin could keep his secret no longer. Blushing with embarrassment, he confided to August that he had been courting the daughter of Dexter Maness, who occupied a nearby claim. August looked at his friend with surprise. Jacob read his thoughts.

"I know what you're going to say, August. She is not of our faith. But we love each other. Should we stay apart because of a difference in faith?"

"I can't answer that, Jacob. Perhaps, though, it would have been better to find a girl of our own people."

"There are none to find," Jacob protested. "August, I shall not forsake our religion. She understands."

"I'm sure of that, Jacob," August said. "And I know that love is a strong thing."

"We will be married in January."

August put his hand on his good friend's shoulder. "So be it, Jacob. It has been a hard year. I'm glad someone around here has found happiness."

Jacob's approaching marriage also brought August to a decision which had been forming throughout the autumn. With the Old Man gone, with Jason out of the territory, with the border raids having quieted down, a wave of restlessness had once again washed over August. Since Jacob's new wife would be able to help with the store, he felt no real ties binding him to the claim.

He and John Grant had been talking about what it would take to get Kansas into the Union as a free state.

"The territory can't last long with two governments," Grant said. "We have our own legislature in Topeka, the slavers have one in Lecompton. And the way the South seems to run Washington, there's too much chance that Congress will decide the Lecompton gang is the one that speaks for the people of Kansas."

"What can I do?" August asked.

"Come along with us," Grant said. "In the spring we've got to talk to every free-stater in the territory. Make them understand what can happen if we don't all get together and turn in such a big vote that Congress has got to take us into the Union as a free state."

"Well, it's not as exciting as dodging grape shot from a cannon. But I think I've had enough of that excitement for a long while."

Eighteen fifty-seven brought a pleasant surprise to August — his parents were in Kansas! They had located him through Theo. When news came that they were on Jacob's claim, August hurried back to Marais des Cygnes for the reunion.

"We have been keeping up with the newspaper reports," said Herz Emmanuel, looking a little grayer but as strong as ever. "It sounded awful out here."

"Well, you know how the newspapers exaggerate," August said, smiling.

He registered a claim for his parents on the creek. Arriving for his first supper in their new home, he saw that on the rough wooden table his mother had laid out the old candlesticks and wine cup.

"This is our first Sabbath together in so long," his mother said. "Our first, but there shall be many more."

August's mother lit the candles. Herz Emmanuel rose and began to repeat the Sabbath prayers, with August joining in. The Hebrew words of the prayers filled the small cabin and the light from the candles shone brightly.

A few weeks later came another unexpected visitor.

"Saw him with my own eyes," Baker said to August. "Camped at Mitchell's claim. The Old Man!"

August headed for the Mitchell claim at a gallop. He followed the dusty wagon trail and reined up in front of the cabin. On the ground he noticed fresh wagon tracks and many footprints. Indoors, a half-extinguished fire smoldered on the crude hearth.

A sound behind him made August turn quickly. It was Mitchell, coming from the creek with a pail of water. "Where is he?" August asked.

Mitchell gave August a strange glance. He set down the pail. "Where's who?"

"The Old Man," August said. "He's here. Baker saw him."

Mitchell stirred the fire. "Baker might have seen wrong."

"He couldn't mistake him," August exclaimed. "He was here. What's wrong? What are you hiding?"

Mitchell looked away. "All right," he said. "It don't make no difference now. Yep, the Old Man was here. He had a wagonload of Negroes with him. He'd helped them escape from Missouri. He's going to run them to Canada, where the slave catchers can't touch them."

"Why didn't anyone come and get me?"

"He made me promise not to get in touch with you," Mitchell said. "He didn't want you to know he was in the territory."

"Didn't want me to know?" August said. "Why wouldn't he want me to know?"

Mitchell shook his head. "He told me you gave up the fight. Said you wouldn't stick with him."

August felt sick. How had the Old Man misunderstood

him so badly?

"Mitchell, listen to me," he said. "The last time I saw him he had a plan to rally a whole army of slaves. He thinks he can end slavery by himself. It was a crazy scheme. It won't work. His ... his mind is not clear. Fred Brown was killed at Osawatomie and I don't think he's gotten over it.

"I think the anti-slavery side is going to win. And it's going to win *peacefully*. That's what I'm working for right now — to make sure Kansas enters the Union as a free state. The Missourians thought they could make slavery legal in the West. They were wrong. They thought if they brought their rifles into Kansas and stole a couple of elections, that would settle the matter. But we gave them the fight of their lives, and we won.

"Now, though, all the Old Man wants to do is attack, attack, *attack!* But the Bible says there is a time for a war, and a time for peace. And this is the time to get things done peacefully. It's true I wouldn't go with him. But I never told him I had given up the fight."

Mitchell was nodding his head slowly.

"Now I understand," he said. "Here's what the old man told me. He's gathering his army. And he's getting ready to strike."

August couldn't believe his ears.

He's really going through with it.

"He'll get killed!" he cried. "Where is he? We need to talk."

"You won't find him," Mitchell said. "When the Old Man means for nobody to find him, ain't no use looking."

One night August heard a muffled sound outside his cabin. He opened the door and there was a man wrapped in a long coat, a broad-brimmed hat pulled down over a shock of blond hair. The man entered swiftly, his left arm swinging uselessly at his side. It was Owen Brown.

"I can't stay long," he told August. "They're hunting us like animals. Wild stories are running around. I wanted you to know the truth. I know you loved him almost as much as we did."

August had been following the story with the rest of the nation. On a fateful night in October 1859, the Old Man had led a small band of armed men, black and white, into Virginia, where they captured the arsenal at Harpers Ferry. They took hostages and barricaded themselves inside the arsenal.

Were they waiting for help to arrive?

The raiders were quickly surrounded by a large force of United States troops, led by Lieutenant Colonel Robert E. Lee. Several of the raiders, including Oliver and Watson Brown, were killed on the spot. Others, including the Old Man, were taken to a military prison. Later, he was sentenced to be hanged.

"He figured the arsenal was the best place to attack

first," Owen began. "We rented a farm on the other side of the river. The Old Man had money enough — more than ten thousand dollars! Got it from some abolitionist people out East. We let on that we were in the livestock business. The Old Man kept buying weapons and storing them away.

"Finally he said we were ready. A lot of free blacks had promised to come along with him. I was supposed to lead them in. But they never came.

"He went in anyway. He told me to wait high up in the woods until the arsenal was theirs. He said the slaves in the area would rush to join the rebellion. 'Give a man a pike and a slave becomes a man,' the Old Man said.

"There was never an army of slaves on its way," Owen said glumly. "At the end there was just a few men ready to die for what they believed in."

" 'No remission of sin without the shedding of blood,' " August said.

"He loved that Bible verse," said Owen sadly. "Maybe that's what the country needs."

"I'm sorry about your father and your brothers," August said, putting his hand on Owen's shoulder.

They embraced. Then Owen Brown wrapped the stained coat around his shoulders and vanished into the night.

HENRIETTA

That winter in the territory was the hardest August had known. The ground lay bare and frozen. Bitter winds rattled through leafless branches, creek beds glittered in motionless ribbons of ice. With little to do around their claims, the settlers holed up and waited for the thaw.

He worked in the store to pass the time. One day his father came in and asked if he would go to Leavenworth and help settle the estate of one of his relatives.

When August arrived in Leavenworth, a family friend from St. Louis, Simon Kohn, was waiting for him.

"You have grown so much!" Simon said. "You look strong, like a man of the country. Nothing like a couple of years fighting the border ruffians, eh?"

"These days, I mostly fight grasshoppers in the field," August joked.

"Your uncle's estate is not a simple one to settle. You will need to be here at least one night."

"That's fine. I'll find a place to rest my head."

Simon shook his head. "No need for that. I have arranged for you to stay the night at the home of George Einstein. He's the city clerk of Leavenworth."

"You didn't need to —"

"— and they are a very nice family. You should get to know them, if you're planning to stay here in Kansas. They are good people to know."

The Einsteins' home was handsome and new. Inside it sparkled with polished woodwork, china, and silverware. August felt uncomfortable about treading on the neat carpets with his boots, but the friendly welcome extended by the city clerk and his wife put him at ease.

They introduced him to Henrietta, their daughter. She was a young, pretty girl with dark hair framing a sensitive face. She smiled and shook his hand.

August just stood there, smiling and gazing at her face. He could not think of a thing to say.

Look away, you fool, he told himself.

That evening, Simon and a few other guests joined them for dinner. Afterward the talk turned to politics.

"We are *not* going to have any more problems with the slaveocracy, I can tell you that," said a bluff, red-faced lawyer named Squire McFarland. "The slavers made their bid for Kansas. They failed! That's why they called a truce. They know they've been beaten. Slaveowning is going out of style. The South just has to accept that."

As the squire rambled on, August's glance turned again to Henrietta. She was glancing at him too.

Suddenly she leaned in and said, "Mr. Bondi, I hear you live in a twelve-foot shanty!"

He was startled. *She speaks!*

"Um, well, I *sleep* in a twelve-foot shanty," he said. "I *live* on the wide open prairie."

"I should like to see where you live, Mr. Bondi."

"Oh, Miss Einstein, you are much better off staying here in Leavenworth," August said, shaking his head. His legs were shaking, too, he noticed. "The border has calmed down some, but it's still no place for a refined young woman like yourself."

"Yet women *are* there, Mr. Bondi, are they not?" Henrietta said.

"W-well, yes," he stammered.

"You know, Mr. Bondi," she said flirtatiously, "it is not just the *men* who decide the future of Kansas. Didn't I hear you say a while ago that those border ruffians would not burn a cabin where there was a woman present? And that an empty cabin would almost certainly be put to the torch?"

"That — that's true," he replied. He felt beads of perspiration forming on the back of his neck.

"Well then," she continued, "if that is the case, then

the only way to ensure that Kansas enters the Union as a free state is to get all of the free-state men married off, wouldn't you say?"

"Well, I, I ..." He stopped. Henrietta's voice and expression had totally flustered him.

The two of them burst into laughter.

"I'm sorry to be so impertinent, Mr. Bondi," she said. "We can talk about something other than politics."

The next day August returned to the settlement. He had planned to help Jacob unload some cases of supplies at the store. Instead, he went riding through the fields. The cracked earth was beginning to show soft green once more. The ground he had plowed at the end of winter had come alive with growing shoots. New life was everywhere. He came to a stop and looked over the prairie, taking in the wonder of creation for a few minutes.

When he returned to the Bondi cabin, his mother looked at him wisely.

"Anschl!" she suddenly said. "You found yourself a *sweetheart* in Leavenworth!"

August blushed.

He told his mother all about Henrietta.

"Are you ready to marry her?" she asked.

"Yes," he said without hesitation.

"When will you ask her?"

"I don't know," he said, looking down at his boots. "I thought of riding back to Leavenworth today. But we hardly know each other. What if I get there and find out she is being courted by another man? Or what if she has no interest in me?"

"You don't have to visit her in person to propose marriage," his mother said cheerfully. "You can *write* her."

Dear Miss Einstein,

I was most delighted to meet you at your parents' house on the first of May. I realize that we have been briefly acquainted, and I beg your forgiveness for any offense this letter may give. I would like very much to ask for the consideration of a proposal of marriage. I would be grateful for the favor of a prompt reply.

With best wishes,
I am,
August Bondi

During the days that followed August waited impatiently and fearfully for his answer. After a week Baker passed by the store and dropped off a small white envelope. The Vermonter winked at him. "Looks like a gal's handwriting to me," he said.

August broke the wax seal and hurriedly unfolded the single sheet. He read through the letter quickly, then again to make sure he had not misunderstood:

Dear Mr. Bondi,
The pleasure of your letter of the third is acknowledged. May I say, Mr. Bondi, that even if I had known you only half as long, my answer to your letter would have been the same. I accept your proposal of marriage and I look forward to future correspondence regarding the arrangements.

Fondly,
Henrietta

This time it was Jacob's turn to slap August on the back and congratulate him: "A family man yet! And a good thing, too."

On their wedding day, the guests crowded into the Einstein house. In the frontier town of Leavenworth there were no materials for a ceremony. Nor was there a rabbi. The benediction was pronounced by Henrietta's uncle. And the glass which August crushed under his boot was one of the last remaining goblets from the Einsteins' china shelf. But Henrietta and August were thrilled.

After the ceremony the guests toasted the new bride and groom. To August it seemed that most of Leavenworth had turned out to shake his hand. Henrietta's uncle also proved himself a very able fiddler, and soon the house rang with the strains of the *freilach*.

Squire McFarland was on hand to register the event in the county records — and carry on some more about the political situation.

"Now see, Bondi, I told you last time you were here that we were on the verge of an era of unprecedented peace. The Kansas question is answered. And the answer is *free state.* It matters not whether Senator Douglas or that hickory splitter Lincoln gets elected president. You know why? Because neither man has the slightest interest in upsetting the Southern states. You wait and see."

"I hope you're right," August said. "The Missourians certainly calmed down once they realized they'd lost the fight."

"That was a great day when the free-state party took over the capital building in Lecompton," said the squire. "Now I know you're wishing the Republicans would just out-and-out abolish slavery, but son, that's not gonna happen. They're good men, these Republicans, but they're *practical* men. They don't want to see slavery spread, but neither do they want to *stir up a war* by forcing the South to give up their slaves!"

The festivities finally came to an end. Everyone said their good-byes, and the newlyweds started back for Marais des Cygnes. The wagon rolled slowly through the rich fields of summer. Henrietta sat alongside August, her face flushed, her bonnet loosely thrown back against her shoulders, her dark hair moving gently in the breeze.

As they neared the settlement, August made out two horsemen in the distance. The riders waved and galloped toward the wagon. The Moore boys. They greeted August and raised their hats to Henrietta.

“They were at Black Jack too, with the Old Man.” August said.

For an instant the old sorrow flooded over him — the memory of the black hills frozen in winter. Then he realized Henrietta was watching him. He smiled. The winter was long over. What he had thought dead was still alive, alive as the grain ripening in the sun.

August slapped the reins on the horse’s back and the wagon moved forward. He turned to Henrietta.

“We’re almost home,” he said.

DIS-UNION

Henrietta began housekeeping in their new cabin. For the first time in his life, August felt willing to settle down. He delighted in watching his bride arrange their sparse furnishings with as much care as if she were still in her home in Leavenworth.

Lately, August had been spending much of his free time helping out one of his new neighbors. Josh Gerth was a lanky young man who looked like a teenager. He always had a battered straw hat balanced on the back of his head. But he had fought bravely alongside August at Osawatomie, and they had become best of friends. Throughout the autumn the two men helped each other lay in provisions and weatherproof their cabins against the cold weather ahead.

Winter came on quickly. And so did the war.

"Squire McFarland couldn't have been more wrong if he had predicted the end of grasshoppers," August said one day at the breakfast table. He was reading his newspaper. It was full of breathless accounts of the secession fever sweeping through the South. Already South Carolina had pulled out of the Union, followed by Mississippi, then Florida, Alabama, Georgia, Louisiana.

"One right after the other," said August. "Six states in the Confederacy, and Texas set to vote on it next week."

"What then?"

"Well, our new president has to decide how important it is to keep these states in the Union."

"They should go," Henrietta said. "They have caused nothing but grief and heartache."

He looked at her. She was beautiful, even when she was upset.

"I've never told you about the first time I saw slaves, have I?"

"Do you mean the time you were in Texas?"

"No, before that. It was my first time setting foot in the country. Our ship was waiting to get towed to New Orleans. We were docked next to a sugar factory. I went inside and saw the slaves working there, eighteen hours a day. They had on gunny sacks for clothes. It made me physically ill."

"August, that's terrible."

He nodded. "My love, answer me this, and be honest."

She looked him intently in the eyes.

"What is it?"

"If you knew that our people were in slavery somewhere in the world, or being mistreated in some way —"

"August Anschl, please," Henrietta said, interrupting him. "I know where you are going with this."

Her eyes began to tear up.

"Sweetheart," he said, taking her hand. "I didn't mean to make you upset. We were just having a discussion."

"Yes," she said bitterly. "A discussion about why you need to go to *war* again!"

"No, my love, no. I do not *need* to go to war again. Young men get excited about war. I have a wife and soon I will have a baby. I am not trying to argue my way into a soldier's uniform."

"There is no war," said Henrietta. "There may never *be* a war."

"Yes, you are right," he said. "I'm sorry I upset you."

The next day, Josh showed up at his door. Jacob, Grant, and Baker were with him.

"Are you coming to the celebration?" Jacob said.

"What celebration?"

"Don't you realize what day it is?" Josh said. "A day for cheering, not working! We aren't a territory any more. We're a state! A free state of the Union!"

"You mean the Dis-Union, don't you?" August said. "I may come along later. Don't wait. I'll try to join you, but don't expect me."

When they had gone Henrietta said, "August, you should be with them. This is what you've worked for ever since you came to the territory."

August nodded. "After I finish some chores," he said.

But there was an ache in his heart, one he hadn't felt in a while. He stood in the doorway and looked across the fields. The cold wind lashed his face.

The Old Man had said there would be greater wars.

There was pounding on the door of the Bondi cabin. August opened it and saw Josh, his hair and eyes wild.

"They've done it!" he shouted. "Looks like we got to teach 'em the same lesson as we taught the ruffians. But I'm game for it. It'll be a real pleasure to settle with those slavers again."

He slapped August on the shoulder.

"We'll join up together again, you and me. Man, I been itchin' for a chance to get my hands on 'em—"

He stopped suddenly and looked at August. "What's wrong? You don't aim to stay out?" His boyishly enthusiastic face turned to one of disappointment.

"We'll go, Josh. I'm not staying out."

"What's the matter, then? Aren't you glad?"

"A war is never anything to be glad about," August said.

After Josh left, August turned and faced Henrietta, who was sitting at the table. He sat across the table from her. For a while they said nothing.

"You will go," she said.

He noticed she hadn't said it as a question.

"I had hoped we could avoid war," August said. "But war we will have. It may be a short one. It may be over by the harvest."

Henrietta looked mournful.

"My love," he continued, "in a few weeks our first child will be born. Let the young men go off to war. I will join them if I am needed. I have fought for freedom all my life. But right now there is much to be done here."

His parents came to live in the cabin. Martha helped Henrietta with the child, a beautiful little girl named Rosa. During the spring and summer August and Herz Emmanuel worked to set the claim in order. He waited anxiously for updates from the war. When they arrived, the news was usually grim. Bull Run, Wilson's Creek, Lexington — all were stinging defeats for the Union army.

Men throughout the North were signing up for the military. That autumn, August made hay, stored up fodder for the livestock, and piled up firewood for winter. He knew he would be signing up, too.

He went to see Jacob and told him that he and Josh Gerth were ready to start for cavalry headquarters in Fort Lincoln.

"I'm not taking you with me this time, Jacob," he said. "Promise me you'll stay behind. Make sure my family can manage."

Jacob shook his hand. "I'll stay here over the winter," he said. "But this is looking to be a long fight."

The dawn broke clear and cold. August saddled his horse. Josh would be waiting for him. Quickly he checked his saddlebags. At the doorway he embraced his parents. His mother wept. Herz Emmanuel put his hand on August's shoulder and tried to smile.

"I have seen you leave us many times," his father said. "I have hoped each would be the last. Perhaps this one will be. Come back safely. May God give you his blessing."

August kissed the child in Henrietta's arms, then drew his wife close to him.

"My blessing, too," she whispered. "And my love."

It was time. August swung into the saddle and rode from the claim. He turned when he reached the top of the hill and looked at the cabin, small in the distance, where his family stood. He raised one hand high. An answering signal of farewell came from the valley.

August turned his horse and headed for Josh Gerth's farm. The hoof beats rang sharply against the earth. He did not look back again.

FIFTH KANSAS

Wearing sergeant's stripes on his arm, August rode beside Josh in the column. Company K had been issued the long-barreled muskets, but the battle-hardened free-state men had sawed down the barrels for a more powerful blast.

"Think we'll ever get to use these?" Josh asked.

"We have plenty of time," August said. "Don't be impatient for trouble."

The trouble came once they reached Arkansas. At Strawberry Creek, August's patrol was met by waves of rebel cavalry. It looked to be about six hundred men.

Company K picketed their horses in the woods and took up positions along the line of trees. The first elements of enemy horsemen galloped across the Kansas flank. The blasts from the free staters' muskets shattered the air. Horses reared and whinnied. Suddenly August saw the field swarm with rebel foot soldiers. Whooping and yelling, they raced across the clearing. The Kansas line held and raked the field with lead.

Face blackened, sweat burning in his eyes, August fired again and again. Beside him, Josh matched shot for shot. The charge wavered and broke. The rebels took cover among the trees on the far side of the field while the smoke of battle drifted over the clearing. A few motionless forms lay on the grass. It had suddenly fallen quiet.

Josh wiped his face with his neckerchief. "Looks like the rebs aim to call it a day."

August's eyes were on the field. "One of them is still alive out there," he said. "Listen."

They listened. Through the still air, acrid with powder smoke, came a faint cry.

"Water!"

Josh shrugged. "Let the rebs take care of him," he said.

"He's closer to our lines," August said. He stood up and raised his musket, butt first, in the air. Josh tried to pull him down but August stepped away. He walked directly toward the clearing and faced the Confederate lines. No signal came from them. August went slowly forward and laid his musket on the ground.

The frightened, wounded soldier looked at him. August knelt and held his canteen to the soldier's lips. He was only a boy, dressed up in a coarse, oversized uniform.

He gulped at the water, then dropped his head back to the ground.

"Much obliged, Yank."

August examined the wound. A bullet had torn into the boy's leg. He ripped a piece of cloth from the soldier's shirt and tried to stop the bleeding. "Where are you from?" August asked while he worked.

"Texas. Come up here to fight the Yanks. Never thought I'd be havin' one take care of me."

"You're a long way from home," August said.

The boy nodded and looked away. "Yep," he said, trying to keep his voice steady. "A long way. Reckon I won't never get back."

"You'll get back," said August.

The Texan raised himself a little. "I never thought a war would be this way. Figgered it'd be more fun than anything. But it ain't. Do you reckon the country's ever going to be together again?"

"Yes," August said. "And I hope it's sooner than later. You boys should have listened to your man Sam Houston when he tried to talk you out of secession."

He beckoned to the gray troops at the edge of the woods. In a few minutes two soldiers cautiously stepped from cover. August drew back while they picked up their comrade. The Texas boy turned once and waved. August walked to Company K's line.

"You coulda got your fool head blown off!" Josh said as August slid down beside him. "And for what? You didn't get any thanks for it. And it sure didn't do the war no good."

Just then from across the field came a rising swell of voices. The Confederates waved their hats and cheered Company K.

Throughout the summer the Fifth Kansas was rarely out of contact with the enemy. There were sharp skirmishes by day and the clash of patrols in the pitch black of night. The column was moving southeast now, driving for the Mississippi River.

Days of rest were seldom, so August treasured them all the more. In camp, he and Josh would sit by the fire, Josh pulling on a stained corncob pipe, August reading and re-reading the letters from Henrietta and his parents. Little Rosa was starting to talk already. He would never recognize her. "But she knows you will come home safe," Henrietta wrote, "and waits for you as I do."

In September, at the time of Rosh Hashanah, August and the three other Jewish soldiers of the Fifth Kansas met for supper. Their table was a piece of canvas laid on the ground and weighted with stones. They had no wine, but one of the men had brought a canteen of hard cider. Army rations of hardtack and salted beef made up the rest of the meal.

In the warm evening the men stretched quietly on the

grass. August studied the faces around him by the light of the tiny campfire. There was Wittenberg, the oldest, with a grizzled mustache and gentle eyes. And there were two Kahn brothers, who farmed near Lawrence.

Wittenberg puffed thoughtfully on his pipe. "Surely some of our own people over there are celebrating this day as we are," he said.

August nodded. "Our people in the South follow the Confederacy. Whether or not they agree in their hearts, their homes are there and they can do little else. War takes no account of a man's religion. Judah Benjamin has a brilliant mind, yet he owns slaves and serves in Jefferson Davis's cabinet. All of us have blind spots that keep us from seeing the whole truth."

"And yet," Wittenberg said, "in days to come our hands may be against them." He sighed. "It is not easy to be a Jew."

"There are times," August added, "when it is not easy to be a man."

He stood and made ready to leave. The soldiers clasped hands.

"May you be inscribed in the Book of Life," Wittenberg said.

"And you — and all of us," said August.

In the distance they heard the artillery start up a night barrage. Soon the Fifth Kansas would be moving forward.

THE LAST CHARGE

Throughout the summer the Fifth Kansas clashed against the strength of an enraged Confederate army. Days of swirling dust, the sharp exchange of musket fire, the watchful nights and bugle calls at dawn. There were new replacements in the company. Captain Harrington lay in a field hospital. Wittenberg's Book of Life had come to its last page near the banks of the Arkansas River. August mourned for the friends he had lost.

During fall and winter the Fifth Kansas occupied Pine Bluff, as the opposing armies caught their breath. The encampment around the little town was quiet. As winter wore away and good weather returned, August and Josh even found a chance to fish and swim. Under a blue sky they felt like boys as they cast their lines into the river.

As the calm lasted it only grew more ominous. There were rumors, always rumors.

Ten thousand rebs are on the march. Price and Shelby are heading for Missouri!

The summer days threatened storms, but the only thunder August heard along the horizon was the booming of cannon.

One morning in September as he swam in the river and felt the cool water flowing around him, he sensed that the days of quiet summer had come to an end. Letters from home only increased his longing to see his family again.

"You know," Josh said, "I never calculated I'd be a marryin' man. But I think now, soon's I get home, I'll find me a wife and settle down. Just hope I'm as lucky as you and it don't take too long."

"I'm sure you will find someone," August said. "Or perhaps someone will find you when you least expect it." He plucked at the grass, recalling that marvelous spring day in Leavenworth. It seemed a lifetime ago.

Josh puffed on his corncob pipe while August closed his eyes a moment, half drowsing. Suddenly the notes of a bugle rang across the fields. They started up and raced toward camp.

Company K was already a mass of soldiers buckling their equipment while the piercing notes of "Boots and Saddles" sounded again and again. August mounted his horse and rode into formation.

The men poured onto the Monticello road at a gallop. Hatless, shirt unbuttoned, Lieutenant Jenkins made his way to the head of the column. The rebels had broken through near Monticello, trying to sever the whole Union line. August passed infantry along the road. Artillery gun-carriages rattled through the dust and the trailing howitzers lurched crazily from side to side.

The troopers rallied in a shallow ditch. Across the fields the sun glinted on rifle barrels, flickered from bayonet points. "Here come the Johnnies!" a rifleman shouted.

"All right, boys," Jenkins cried. "We can hold the rebs! That's all we have to do. Hold 'em! The rest of the brigade's coming up from Pine Bluff."

The artillery carriages crashed through the bushes on the left.

August turned to Josh. "I guess we can keep them busy for half an hour," he said.

Josh wiped his face. "That line can't hold ten minutes!"

The rebel troops were in sight, moving to Company K's flank. Then suddenly August saw the Confederate cavalry bearing down on the Union forces. The howitzer batteries opened fire. Minie balls ripped viciously through the air.

"Stand fast!" Jenkins shouted. The rebel horsemen were nearly upon them.

Now!

Company K's bugle sounded a wild charge. August and Josh plunged forward. The troops met in opposing waves, in a sea of rearing horses. August tried to fight his way through. A rebel horseman swung at him with a saber, then dropped from his saddle as August fired his pistol point blank.

The Confederates wheeled to disengage. In the welter of horses and shouting men August saw Josh slump in his saddle. He caught him before he could fall off. Then his own mount shuddered and pitched forward. The Minie ball fire increased. August stumbled clear and pulled Josh from the trampling hoofs around them.

Josh's face was pale and drenched with sweat. His eyes wavered as he looked at August. A faint smile and boyish expression crossed his face. "Won't have time for Kansas after all," he whispered.

"You'll be all right," August said. "We'll get you out."

Josh Gerth shook his head. "No use. Let me be." A widening stain of red covered his shirt.

August rushed back to join the infantry. There was no time to grieve his fallen friend.

The Confederates kept up the attack. The Union line swayed and buckled. Further down a howitzer exploded. The rebel small-arms fire bit into the column. A section of infantry had been pushed back and carried August with it. He shouldered his way forward.

He saw Sergeant Major Denton clutch his head and spin wildly. Jenkins was down. Parker, the bugler, lay with his leg shattered. The line was breaking.

A cold rage seized August. He sprang to a riderless

horse and trampled his way into the crowd of infantry. "Get back in line!" he shouted. "Back!"

The infantry halted. August could barely hear his own voice and knew only that he was shouting at them. His head pounded and his eyes were blinded with sweat. The riflemen moved slowly into position again.

He galloped back and forth along the line. The howitzers had begun again, but the rebel riflemen were gathering for another attack. Enemy horsemen still occupied the draw.

August wheeled to rejoin his company. Shadowy figures were racing across the field in front of him through curtain of smoke. Shouts of attacking men mingled with rifle fire. Searing pain suddenly filled his chest and stomach and took his breath away. Another impact threw him from the saddle.

As he fell, the reins slipped from his hand. The hard ground came up to meet him. Overhead the treetops circled dizzily and the horizon disappeared. The sun turned black.

It was quiet when August opened his eyes. Under a blazing sky motionless shapes of men and horses covered the field. Pain flooded his body. The sun crushed him like a burning weight. He ran his tongue over his parched, blackened lips and fumbled for the canteen. It was gone. He called feebly. The hoarse rattle of his voice seemed to come from a great distance. No answer. The silence of the dead.

The sun beat mercilessly. August tried vainly to drag himself toward the line of trees. He could not move. He bit his wrist to ward off the pain dragging him into unconsciousness. For a strange moment he thought himself back in Marais des Cygnes. She was waiting in the cabin. He called to her.

Henrietta! Over here! I'm ...

The dream lifted suddenly and he understood where he was. Josh lay somewhere on the field. And Jenkins. And Denton. August felt his strength ebbing. He fought against the shadows that dropped over his eyes. Everything was fading.

His lips attempted to form the words of the Hebrew prayer.

"*Shema Yisroel ... adonoy eloheynu ... adonoy ... echod ...*"

Then darkness.

HOME

There were voices. Water on his lips. Someone was holding a canteen to his mouth. August gasped and sputtered. He was breathing hard. His whole body felt like it was on fire.

He opened his eyes painfully and looked up on a bearded face beneath a gray campaign hat.

"Well, Yank," the Confederate said, "it looks like you ran into a little trouble."

August heard someone else say, "He's bad off, Cap'n. No use takin' him prisoner."

"Listen, Yank," said the Captain, "your boys are picking up casualties under a flag of truce. You think you can hold out a little while?"

August nodded.

The officer left the canteen within his reach and walked on. The sergeant propped a pair of boots under August's head. He closed his eyes. The pain was excruciating.

More footsteps. He opened his eyes to see three teenagers with rifles. They were smirking.

"Wouldn't you rather be home right now, Yank?" one of them asked him.

August looked at him sorrowfully.

"Wouldn't *you?*" he asked.

One of the others slapped his pal on the back. "Yank is right!" he said.

"Hey Yank," the third one said. "You got any money?"

"I need it more than you do," August replied.

He closed his eyes. *Take it if you want it. I don't care.*

He heard them walk away.

After what seemed like hours he heard noises. He looked around. A detail of Union soldiers was picking their way through the field. August raised one hand weakly. Two stretcher-bearers came toward him.

"What's your outfit?" one of them asked.

"Fifth Kansas."

The stretcher-bearer nodded. "We're Twenty-Eighth Wisconsin. The rest of your boys are back in Pine Bluff. You did a pretty good job today."

"Did we hold out long enough?" August asked.

"Sure did," the Wisconsin man said. "Stopped 'em right here. I know for a while we were all scared the division was going to be cut in half. But you and your boys gave us time to work our way around. Anyway, you don't need to worry about all that. Looks like you aren't going to have any more war for a long time."

A jolting wagon carried August to the field hospital. As he was carried into the tent, he saw rows and rows of cots, all filled with soldiers. A tall man serving as the nurse put makeshift bandages on his wounds, then moved on to the next soldier.

Late that night the ward surgeon looked at August briefly.

"Tell me the truth," August asked. "What are my chances?"

The surgeon shook his head. "How can anybody know his chances? All I can tell you is this: don't give up. The hospital's as big a battle as the field. We have nothing. There's not six clean sponges in the outfit. One nurse to a ward — and the ward gets bigger every day. We'll treat you as well as we can. But you've got to help yourself."

The next day when the ward nurse came by for the bandage change, he avoided eye contact with August. Finally, August asked, "What have you heard?"

The nurse stopped wrapping the bandage. He looked at August. Then he told him what the surgeon had said.

"He said the wound is very serious. He's not sure you will survive."

"As God wills," August said. "But I believe I shall live."

The tent was unbearably hot by midday. Flies and mosquitoes hovered overhead. His cot was infested with lice and maggots. The food was inedible. He refused shots of morphine, choosing instead to suffer.

The pain is keeping me alive.

He asked for his head and beard to be shaved, which helped with the lice. He started to feel better. He dressed his own wounds. It was early November before he could walk again, but once on his feet he knew his strength would soon return.

To keep himself busy he helped the army nurses on their rounds. Company K had moved on. The ward surgeon told August he would not be returned to duty. As soon as he was well enough he would go home. He had been gone three years.

In November he was well enough to leave the field hospital. An ambulance driver offered him a ride to Little Rock. From there he made his way to Memphis and a riverboat.

As he sat on deck watching the shoreline slowly pass by, he thought back to his first journey up the Mississippi River. It was just after he told his father he was changing his name to August.

Anschl is back in Vienna, Father. There with his comrades. Defending freedom.

I hope someday Anschl is able to join us here, Herz Emmanuel had said.

August shut his eyes to doze a little. His thoughts drifted to Henrietta and their three-year-old daughter.

Rosa won't recognize her Papa, he thought.

Suddenly the ship's whistle blew. His eyes opened. Instinctively he looked up at the pilot house. In the shadows was the profile of a barrel-chested man navigating the boat. August sat up and looked again.

Is that Chubb?

The sailor stepped out of the pilot house. It was not Chubb. Just seeing a man who reminded him of the captain, however, stirred something in August. He shut his eyes again. Memories of the *Brazos* came flooding back.

I like a boy that ain't scared of a little excitement.

Drop anchor! Drop anchor if you don't want to get blown halfway to Houston!

We'll make a sailor out of you yet, greenhorn.

Massa, I surely thought you was different than the rest.

I hate to lose you, son.

From the riverboat August transferred to the new rail line that crossed Missouri. Once he reached Kansas, he reported to the Army base and received his discharge papers. Now it was time for the slow trek home.

He rode past the old claim. Kansas was the thirty-fourth state in the Union, but this stretch of farmland would always be "the territory" to him.

Sir, if you happen to know any free-state folk, you tell 'em they need to take a stand.

You're gonna need a lesson like the one we gave Baker!

We don't call him the Old Man to his face. He's our father.

I delivered the poor that cried, and the fatherless, and him that had none to help him.

And Kansas is only the beginning, Bondi.

August stopped in his tracks. Tears came to his eyes.

The Old Man was right. He was righter than he knew.

He approached the crest of the hill.

He had left the settlement during this same season of bare trees and barren ground. But he knew the hard earth was alive, deep under its shell of frost. The green of the future was invisible — but it was there, growing, waiting to ripen.

He dismounted and stood on the hilltop for a while. As he watched the cabin below he saw a figure emerge. A little girl.

"Rosa!" He called to her and waved.

The girl stopped, looked up, then hurried back inside.

His heart leaped.

Other figures appeared in the doorway. He waved again, then started down the hill.

August Bondi (1833-1907) fully recovered from his Civil War wounds and went on to live a long and interesting life, mostly in the Kansas town of Salina. He worked as a farmer, a journalist, a businessman, and town postmaster. At age sixty-three he passed the bar examination and was elected a probate judge. The Bondis were the parents of nine children.

On the fiftieth anniversary of the Vienna uprising, he returned to Austria and laid a wreath at the grave of Heinrech Spitzer, his friend and fellow member of the Academic Legion.

Today, August Bondi's role in creating the free state of Kansas is remembered at the Black Jack Battlefield, a National Historic Landmark located near Baldwin City, Kansas.

ABOUT THIS BOOK

Because August Bondi was deeply involved in three major struggles for freedom — the 1848 revolutions, Bleeding Kansas, and the Civil War — his story has long fascinated readers of American history. After his death in 1907, his children published *The Autobiography of August Bondi*. It was immediately hailed as one of the best accounts of the Bleeding Kansas period. There was a revival of interest in Bondi after the Holocaust, when people were taking a fresh look at heroes in Jewish history. The *Autobiography* was turned into a musical piece called *A Ballad of August Bondi* in 1955 and a novel for young readers, *Border Hawk,* published in 1958.

Lloyd Alexander (1924–2007) had been assigned to write *Border Hawk*, even though he had never published a youth novel before. After *Border Hawk,* he went on to write forty more books for young readers and won two of the highest honors in literature, the Newbery Medal and the National Book Award.

I discovered *Border Hawk* in 2006, and after reading it I

called the author to tell him how much I enjoyed it. The book was out of copyright, and we had a conversation about our company, Quindaro Press, reissuing *Border Hawk*. Eventually, though, I decided to rewrite the text of the book so that August Bondi's amazing story would speak to readers today.

For *Firebrand,* I started with the manuscript of *Border Hawk.* Lloyd Alexander's storyline was faithful to the account in the *Autobiography of August Bondi,* and his action scenes gave the story pace and energy. I added a great deal of dialogue and revised the existing dialogue. I changed some descriptions to make them more historically accurate, and I added a number of scenes based on accounts I had read in the *Autobiography.* If you are interested in learning more about how I turned *Border Hawk* into *Firebrand*, I have posted the details to the Quindaro Press website.

My wife, Diane Eickhoff, was my sounding board and cheering section, as she always is. Without her I could not have brought this book to completion.

—*A.B.*

ABOUT THE AUTHOR

Aaron Barnhart was a nationally syndicated media and television critic for *The Kansas City Star.* Along with his wife Diane Eickhoff, he lives in Kansas City, Missouri. They speak widely on the humanities and run a publishing company together. Aaron also manages the Rainbow Community Garden at the church they attend in Kansas City, Kansas.

Q
QUIN
DARO